THE
STAR
IN THE
FOREST

by MARTHA BENNETT STILES

THE
STAR
IN THE
FOREST

a mystery of
the dark ages

FOUR WINDS PRESS   NEW YORK

LIBRARY OF CONGRESS CATALOGING IN PUBLICATION DATA

Stiles, Martha Bennett.
  The star in the forest.

  Summary: Near the end of the sixth century, the daughter of a
Gallic lord witnesses what she believes to be the murder of her
brother and the beginning of a plot to usurp her father's title
  [1. Gaul—Fiction.   2. France—History—To 987—Fiction]
I. Title.
PZ7.S8557Ss   [Fic]   78-22284
ISBN 0-590-07537-3

PUBLISHED BY FOUR WINDS PRESS
A DIVISION OF SCHOLASTIC MAGAZINES, INC., NEW YORK, N.Y.
COPYRIGHT © 1979 BY MARTHA BENNETT STILES
PRINTED IN THE UNITED STATES OF AMERICA
LIBRARY OF CONGRESS CATALOG CARD NUMBER: 78-22284
1 2 3 4 5 83 82 81 80 79

To Ellen and Shirley Emerson,
and to Christina, Aleta, and Barbara Nordman,
who have helped me
on more manuscripts than this one

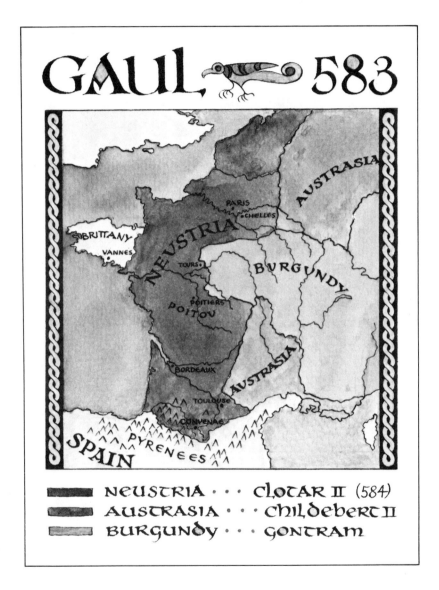

GAUL 583

NEUSTRIA · · · CLOTAR II (584)
AUSTRASIA · · · CHILDEBERT II
BURGUNDY · · · GONTRAM

Places labeled on map: PARIS, CHELLES, BRITTANY, VANNES, TOURS, POITIERS, POITOU, BORDEAUX, TOULOUSE, CONVENAE, PYRENEES, SPAIN, NEUSTRIA, AUSTRASIA, BURGUNDY

Background

THE BRONZE AGE INHABITANTS OF THE LANDS WE CALL FRANCE and the Romans called Gaul seem to have been a dark, fleet-footed race called Ligurians. Centuries before Julius Caesar came (in 51 B.C.), they had lost all of their territory except perhaps the forest depths to tribes of larger men.

From 51 B.C., Gaul was part of the Roman empire for 350 years, during which time Latin became the language of these conquering tribes—now called Gallo-Romans— and Roman Catholicism became their religion.

In the fifth century, Rome lost the power to control her empire. Various Germanic tribes, chiefly the Arian Visigoths and the pagan Franks, warred with each other and with the Gallo-Romans for control of the territories of Gaul from which the Roman legions were withdrawing. The victor was the Frankish king Clovis, who in 496 had stopped fighting long enough to decree that all his people should become Roman Catholic on the instant. [Even as late as 583, however—the date that the story of *The Star in the Forest* begins—few Franks spoke Latin, and memories of the old gods, like Odin (also called the One-eyed god, the Spear-lord, the Host-Father) were not entirely lost.]

Clovis's decree was a major reason for the Franks' success, for they were the only important Germanic invaders of Gaul who converted to the native church. Gallo-Roman churchmen, forced to choose among conquerors, naturally supported the Franks: Gallo-Roman territory conquered by Franks retained its native church hierarchy, while territory conquered by other

Barbarians did not. (In 583, most of Gaul's bishops were still Gallo-Roman—or, as their Frankish conquerors called Gallo-Romans, "Roman.")

By 507 Clovis had driven the Visigoths into Spain and made himself king of territories corresponding roughly to modern France. (Brittany remained independent and pagan.) Due to the Frankish custom of dividing a man's property among his surviving sons, by 583 Clovis's Gaul was split into three, frequently warring kingdoms: Burgundy and Neustria, ruled by two of Clovis's grandsons, and Austrasia, ruled by their thirteen-year-old nephew Childebert II. In 583, a third, disinherited, grandson of Clovis's was in refuge on a Mediterranean island, after failing in an attempt to seize "his share" of Gaul. This Pretender to the Throne's attempt had been financed by the Byzantine emperor, in the hope of establishing a king in Gaul who, owing him everything, would do as he said.

The Pretender's existence was a sword hanging over the head of everyone in Gaul.

Names

Ancient Frankish names contained more crude breathy sounds than their modern versions. The name of Chlotvech (from *Chlodo,* meaning "renowned," plus *vech,* "warrior," or "priest"), who became king of the Franks in 481, was probably spoken by his subjects as a growl followed by an expectoration. These Franks would be astounded to see Chlotvech rendered in its modern form of "Louis" (assuming they could read, which would be the wrong assumption almost every time). In between "Chlotvech" and "Louis" came a succession of modifications, of which I have chosen the one most commonly used nowadays for Gaul's conqueror, Clovis.

So many of Clovis's descendants had names beginning with that same growl that readers would have difficulty keeping them straight if I did not deliberately spell names inconsistently. Therefore I have named, for example, a miller's son the modern "Luther," while spelling his sovereign of the same name in the older way, "Clotar." (Older still would have been "Chlotar.")

Major Fictional Characters

ALARIK ALANSSON: A Frank, born 565, in Poitou, an area in what is now western France and was then western Neustria. Because Alarik owns no land he has commended himself to Eurik, Lord of Poijou. This means that Alarik tenant-farms a portion of Lord Eurik's villa, Poijou, and in return follows Lord Eurik in any wars to which Eurik rides, on the side Eurik chooses.

ANTONIA: Poijou Villa's midwife, a Gallo-Roman slave.

BERTO: In 583, sole surviving legitimate son of Eurik of Poijou.

BRUNEHAUT: Orphaned daughter of a Frankish lord; foster-daughter of Lord Eurik of Poijou; foster-sister of Eurik's son Berto and daughter Valrada.

CHRONA: Wife of Eurik of Poijou; mother of Berto and Valrada; foster-mother of Brunehaut.

CLAUDIA: A freed Gallo-Roman maidservant to Lady Chrona of Poijou.

DAG: Lord of Antier, a fictional villa in Poitou immediately west of the ancient highway from Spain to Tours and immediately north of Poijou, the (also fictional) villa of Dag's brother Eurik. Dag and Eurik's grandfather entered Gaul in Clovis's army and won his land for his part in expelling the Visigoths from Poitiers. Dag and Eurik have fought their last several campaigns for the king of Neustria.

DEACON: In sixth-century Gaul, one rank below priest. Antier's deacon is a Gallo-Roman.

DOMNOLA: Breton captive bought by Lady Chrona of Poijou. Bretons were the inhabitants of Brittany, often at war with their neighbors the Franks.

ERMAN OF NIORT: One of the six brothers-in-law of Dag of Antier.

EURIK: Lord of Poijou; only brother of Dag of Antier; father of Berto and Valrada.

LEHUN: Lord of Claigne; like Dag, Erman, and Eurik, a Frankish oathman of the king of Neustria—that is, he holds his land in return for following the king to war on demand. Claigne bounds Dag's Antier on the north.

LUTHER OF THE BOURRE: Son of a Frankish miller of Poitou.

MARK: Lord of Vien, the villa lying immediately south of Poijou; a Frank.

NICOLAUS: Poijou's physician; a Greek.

RIKIMER: Sole surviving legitimate son of Dag of Antier.

ULDIN: Frankish oathman of the king of Neustria; one of the six brothers-in-law of Dag of Antier.

VALRADA: Daughter of Lord Eurik and Lady Chrona of Poijou.

WULF: Eldest son of Lehun of Claigne.

Nonfictional Characters

AGNES, MOTHER: Abbess of the Monastery of the Holy Cross (Ste. Croix) of Poitiers, 5??-587.

CHILDEBERT II (570-596): King of Austrasia, 575-596; great-grandson of Clovis: nephew of Gontram of Burgundy.

CLOTAR I (497-561): Last surviving son of Clovis; king of Gaul, 558-561.

CLOTAR II (584-628): Great-grandson of Clovis; cousin of Childebert of Austrasia; nephew of Gontram of Burgundy. Clotar became king of Neustria in the year of his birth, after the assassination of his father.

CLOVIS (465-511): A Frank who became his people's king at the age of sixteen and led them in their conquest of Gaul, requiring them to adopt the religion (Roman Catholicism) of Gaul's native population along the way.

GONTRAM: Born no later than 534; Gontram became King of Burgundy on the death of his father, Clotar I.

JUSTINA, SISTER: Prioress of Ste. Croix in the late sixth century; Gallo-Roman.

PRETENDER, GONDOBALD THE (5??-585): Clovis's dynastic successors were called Merovings. Alone among Catholics, Merovings were allowed as many wives as they liked. Alone among male Franks, they might leave their hair uncut, and neither braided nor bound. According to Frankish law, females did not inherit land, but legitimate sons divided their father's land equally. The heirs to a Meroving's kingdom were those sons whose hair he had permitted to grow uncut. Gondobald the Pretender was the disowned son of Clotar I. Gondobald's long hair was sheared by his father and twice more by his royal half-brothers, but each time he escaped confinement. The Byzantine Emperor sheltered him until 582, when he was brought back to Gaul by Austrasian-Burgundian conspirators to fight for a kingdom in Gaul. King Gontram of Burgundy discovered the conspiracy and the Pretender fled to a Mediterranean island, to try again in 584.

RADEGONDA (Ste. Radegund) (521-587): Thuringian princess, captured by the Franks and forced to become the fourth (concurrent) wife of Clotar I. Radegonda deserted her crown for the veil after Clotar, having heard that her brother was plotting a rebellion, had him murdered. Radegonda founded the Monastery of the Holy Cross (Ste. Croix) at Poitiers, where she remained until her death.

THE
STAR
IN THE
FOREST

I

ON A SUNNY JUNE DAY IN THE YEAR OF GRACE 583, VALRADA, daughter of Lord Eurik of Poijou, happened to look down Poijou Hall's stairs and see her only living brother strolling across the forehall, his quiver swinging gently at his waist. "Berto!"

The quiver began to swing more briskly. "I haven't much time, Val. My horse is saddled already."

Valrada caught up with him before he could get through the door. "I'd much rather ride with you than weave on a day like this. Do wait while they saddle one for me."

"You wouldn't get much of a ride. I'm only going to the far meadow. We're going to shoot."

She followed him into the courtyard, keeping her face resolutely toward the stable so as not to have to acknowledge his frown. "I'll race you there."

Valrada had assumed that Berto's "we" meant that their cousin Rikimer would be meeting him, and so of course Rikimer's deacon, but there were three men waiting in the shade of their horses. Valrada recognized the extra man; he was one of those who had followed her father to war in Brittany. She knew this one because her father had sent for him when a bull had gored Berto's colt. Alarik. Alarik *Whose*son? Nobody special, some freeholder; Valrada couldn't remember.

Rikimer's gaunt face was expressionless as he returned Valrada's greeting, but the deacon made a pseudo-jesting remark to Berto about crowing hens. Berto looked uncomfortable. Why he cared more for some shaven-pated deacon's feelings than for hers was a question Valrada knew there was no use asking him.

"Good morning," Alarik said, and Valrada realized with startled gratitude that he was speaking to her.

He was taller than Berto and her father; as tall as Rikimer, but burlier. Valrada did not like brittle men. There was a nondescript dog lying across one of his feet; he eased it off when he saw her looking at it. The dog had probably followed him from home, Valrada guessed—uninvited like herself.

"How far is that target?" Berto asked.

"Ride it off yourself," the deacon said.

That she needed help dismounting would not have occurred to Valrada's brother or cousin, or to Valrada herself, but as her toes touched stubble, Alarik was at her bridle.

"I will," Berto answered the deacon.

Rikimer shrugged, then spurred his stud to follow Berto.

Alarik and Valrada looked at each other and laughed.

In the bright sky little shepherdless clouds roamed as they pleased. A meadowlark embraced all he saw with exultant song, answered, answered, and answered by his kindred. Now and then the wind flattened the uncut grass in the far end of the meadow, and it shone.

"What's the dog's name?" Valrada asked.

The deacon spat, commented in Latin to his horse, and trotted off after Berto and Rikimer.

"Lahm." Lahm's tail wagged tentatively.

He was lame, Valrada saw. She bent and patted the dismayingly ugly head. "He looks clever."

Alarik smiled. After a moment's silence Valrada asked,

"How old is Lahm?" This was a careful rephrasing of what she had nearly asked—"Is he full-grown?"—because that might indicate some feeling on her part that Lahm should grow bigger; might contain, if Lahm would not grow bigger, some implication that Lahm was a runt.

"He was whelped last fall."

There had to be something else she could ask about the dog. She studied the creature, aware that Alarik was studying her. Her heart raced, while her mind seemed to be slogging through mud.

"You ride well," Alarik said. "When we first saw the two of you, I thought for a minute it was Lord Eurik with Berto."

"Not he. Didn't swords and lances drive Gothic bowmen out of these very fields?"

Alarik laughed.

They were still grinning at each other when the other three came thudding back.

Valrada had forgotten to watch, but she could hear in Rikimer's "Now can we begin?" that he had had to move the target. On top of that, Berto drew first ride.

"What are *you* going to do?" the deacon needled Valrada.

"Lady Valrada can judge our scores," Alarik interposed.

Valrada mounted immediately, to make it harder for Berto to veto Alarik.

Berto glanced uncomfortably at Rikimer, but kept silent.

Valrada looked demurely at her reins. "I know it's hard," her mother was incessantly telling her, "but you must learn this. A man who demands more, gets more. A girl who demands more, gets less." A few years ago

Valrada would have demanded to compete with Berto and Rikimer, and often as not they wouldn't even have let her stay and watch.

A sheep bleated at the far end of the meadow and a crow flew away to the forest, cawing. With a yell that made Valrada's horse jump, Berto spurred his dun and charged the target.

It looked to Valrada as if Berto's first arrow fell short and the eleventh wide—shooting backward was harder— but nine out of twelve was a good score. She glanced at Alarik and he nodded.

Rikimer's horse seemed to burst into full gallop almost from standing. One of the little clouds passed across the sun, as if the sky blinked. "That stud was sired by the wind," Alarik muttered.

"He's fast, but he's stupid," Valrada said. "My cousin has to feed him with a bit in his mouth to keep him from choking himself to death."

Alarik patted the black gelding's neck.

Rikimer had loosed six arrows exactly by the time he was abreast of the target, and now over his shoulder his bow gave wings to six more in just the same space. Twelve times the target jumped like a staked prisoner.

At the far end of the meadow, all the sheep began to call.

"You're next," the deacon prodded.

"Get back, Lahm," said Alarik. "Stay."

If any of Alarik's shafts had missed, Valrada would have lost interest in him.

Lahm, disobeying, followed the black gelding a few feet, then stood looking after it. As Alarik reined in beyond the target and the deacon chose his first arrow, Lahm's body stiffened. His muzzle wrinkled, his ruff lifted, and a low growl began in his throat.

"Keep still, you filthy mutt," snapped the deacon, fighting his horse.

Lahm's growl erupted.

The three men beyond the target began to shout, then wheeled and tore northward. One of the sheep was down, and a gray shape was streaking toward the forest.

Valrada's first glimpse of the wolf was her last.

The forest swallowed them all.

Rikimer reined in first. The others quickly joined him, in a little clearing beside a new-fallen oak. They were all wet and winded. "It's useless without dogs," Rikimer said.

"Oh, we have a fine dog," the deacon panted. From somewhere behind them came Lahm's intermittent yaps.

Alarik regarded the deacon with no change of expression. Valrada wished Berto would put the Roman in his place.

"Yes, that's quite an animal you've got." Berto produced a laugh, and glanced at Rikimer.

Suddenly Lahm's barking was quite near. A doe broke out of the underbrush, Lahm behind her. She did not, Valrada thought, even see the men as she leaped the fallen oak and ran across the clearing in front of them.

"*Down*, Lahm, *stay!*" Alarik commanded, and Lahm dropped. The doe dropped in the same instant, the deacon's arrow quivering in her spine.

Even Rikimer looked startled. There was no sound but Lahm's whining. Alarik, without turning his head, watched Berto. Berto looked sideways at Rikimer. The doe's forelegs struggled. She lifted her head, trying to see the dog. Her great liquid eyes stared straight into Valrada's.

The deacon made no move. Looking at none of them,

Alarik fitted an arrow and sent it into the doe's neck.

The deacon dismounted and walked over to the carcass.

Valrada meant her voice to be outraged, but it was half sobbing. "We don't kill does in calving time!"

The deacon plunged his knife into the doe's neck. "I thought it was a stag."

"Who ever saw a hornless stag in June?" The words came in spite of Valrada. Already at her first outburst Alarik and Berto had begun to scrutinize their horses' manes, and Rikimer was looking at her with one eyebrow lifted.

"Either way," the deacon dragged the doe toward the fallen oak, "the meat's as good." He hoisted the doe onto the dead tree trunk, toppled her onto her back, and spread her hind legs.

"See," said Valrada, "she did have a calf. Look at her bag."

Looking Valrada straight in the eye, the deacon ripped the doe the length of her belly.

Dimly, Valrada heard Rikimer speak, Berto answer. The deacon tossed Lahm the paunch. Valrada's eyes had not left the deacon's knife. Without wiping it he laid it on the fallen oak and bent over to grope for the doe's heart. "We'll have to look for the calf," Valrada said.

Berto groaned. Alarik sat very still, his eyes moving from brother to sister. It was the first time he had looked at her, Valrada was acutely conscious, since the doe had dropped.

She slid down from her horse.

"We have to get this carcass home before it stiffens," Berto reminded her.

"Not it—she." Valrada tied her horse to a tree.

Rikimer dismounted.

Valrada would show neither surprise nor gratitude.

"She broke cover just about there," she told Rikimer, pointing.

He smiled at her politely. Taking the deacon's horse by the bridle, he led it over beside the gutted doe.

Alarik was also dismounting, but though his face was sympathetic, Valrada saw that he was only after his dog. She felt her chin tremble. "It can't be far from here. She must have been with it when Lahm started her."

"You know that may not be so, Val," Berto answered. "And the meat may spoil as it is. We're miles from——"

"He knew it was June when he shot," Valrada cried. "He knew how far we...how...and he knew," she rounded on the deacon, "he knew it was a doe!"

The reins moved in Berto's hands, back and forth. The deacon wiped the sweat from his forehead with a bloody sleeve. "Your little sister credits me with knowing a good deal," he observed. "Almost as much as she knows herself." Berto flushed.

"It will die," Valrada pled as Rikimer and the deacon remounted. "It will starve."

Alarik scooped Lahm up. "It won't linger," he lied to her. "The foxes will find it tonight. They'll kill it quickly."

Valrada stared up at all of them. "If you won't search, then go."

"Fair enough," said Rikimer, and clucked to his stallion.

The deacon laughed and followed.

"Come on, Val," muttered Berto.

She could not read Alarik's face as he rode away.

Flies were thick where the doe had bled and the offal stank—also one of the men might look back. Valrada stalked well out of the clearing before sitting down and bursting into tears. This Alarik who seemed so kind had not even left her his dog. Men were sheep—those who weren't wolves. Valrada's head lifted with a jerk that sent fire through her neck. The wolf they had chased would still be bloody from its kill. She had no weapon.

Opposite her in the underbrush something rustled.

II

June 583, Same day

Rikimer led. Behind Berto the doe's carcass bounced on the deacon's horse, blood surging at each jar. In Alarik's arms Lahm was stiff with attention.

Alarik held the dog tightly. It would not have been able to sniff out the fawn; a new fawn had no smell. No dog, no merciful fox, would find it.

The deacon commented behind Berto, "I never saw a horse so slow it couldn't keep out of its own way."

Alarik could just hear Berto's sullen answer. "It's yours that gets thwacked hideless if we go faster."

Only Alarik, besides Lahm, saw the rabbit start from the brush and dash for new cover. Churning frantically, the dog scrambled out of Alarik's arms and leaped to earth. The other three riders glanced back.

"He may have scented wolf again." Alarik turned Storm as he spoke. "I'll catch up with you."

"You don't mean to hunt wolf alone?" Rikimer asked.

"Oh, he has that three-legged Sirius," said the deacon.

Alarik looked past him to Rikimer. "I'll mark its lair and come back with my brother and his pack." He let his eyes slide back momentarily to Berto's. The gratitude in them was palpable.

She sat on a carpet of white petals, her back against a tree trunk wide as a throne. The fawn lay in her lap.

He had expected her to be relieved, but the light in her eyes was pure pride. She smiled up at him without moving and he was overtaken by a sensation of a spinning sinking that left him weak. He could not speak, and she did not. He dismounted.

She bent her head over the tiny dappled fawn. Her hair fell down across her face, exposing her neck. The feeling of being sucked in a downward spiral swirled him again and he steadied himself on Storm's neck. The horse stood unnaturally, not blinking, even nostrils and tail stone still.

The small clearing where she sat was bathed in a dim green light. He was as conscious of being outside her space as if he stood beyond the reaches of the light of a fire. He imagined himself standing at the mouth of a grotto which by reason of enchantment he might not enter. Ferns raised feathery behind her like seaweed in the still, cool depths of the ocean. A shaft of green-moted gold from some tiny gap in the forest ceiling turned the top of her lowered head to red-gold; then she lifted her face to him again.

He swallowed with an effort and took a step toward her. One arm, like her neck white as if it had never seen sunlight, had slipped free of its sleeve nearly to the elbow, circling her sleeping prize. She gave no sign of rising as Alarik approached. He dropped beside her.

If she had been any but his lord's daughter, he would have reached for her without a word.

Sweat, at that suffocating picture, and at those that followed, started on his forehead. He stared hard at the fawn, trying to think.

There were rockroses growing in the slight space

between them, and quaking grass pushed its way between the roses and the tree's scattered blossoms.

He was acutely conscious of his breathing.

Her hand, long and slender, rested lightly on the fawn's neck. Brown sides moved softly in and out above her thighs. He stroked the dark line down the little animal's spine; instantly her hand withdrew. With his own he picked up a fallen horse-chestnut petal: "Spotted, like him," he said.

She brushed her hair back to look at what he held; she leaned slightly toward him. His heart lurched.

Its painful jerk, as if it would leave his body, reminded him of Lahm. Inevitably, the rabbit hunt proving futile, Lahm would return to the doe's offal. Any minute they would hear him. Alarik rolled the petal between his fingers and squeezed it small. Lord Eurik had good dogs, only good dogs. "Your cousin rides a fine horse," he said abruptly.

"Too nervous," she answered. "For all its stuffs, it stays bony. It suits Rikimer, but I doubt if it could bear your weight."

He looked at her and she dropped her gaze and bent her head so that her hair shielded her face again. He couldn't tell what she was thinking. His ears burned.

"What do you call yours?"

She wanted to know what he called his horse. "Storm. His name is Storm. I had a stallion, before. This——" he broke off as the notes of a bird chimed crystal from the forest. She held her head away from him, listening.

"Nightingale," she whispered.

"Nightingales don't sing this late in the summer. That's a thrush."

She listened spellbound, scarcely a hand's distance from

him. He blessed the bird for its trills and runs, so numerous and so certain all to be repeated.

He wanted to give her something. He broke off one of the rockroses; its stamens spread out at the pressure of his fingers, the golden tuft opening to his touch. He had never thought about that before. He was careful not to look at her. The bird at last fell still. "It sings that way when rain's coming," he told her, afraid that silence would let her collect her thoughts and leave him.

"Then we must go."

He could have bloodied his knuckles against the tree for his stupidity. He made himself jump to his feet and take the fawn from her.

She let him help her mount, but her face flushed. Lahm bounded up, graceless tail wagging. He sniffed the fawn all over, grave as a bachelor uncle, and seemed to know that he would be expected to get home on his own feet. Alarik took the fawn in front of him on Storm's back and promised, before he parted from her, what he knew would be in the end impossible.

III

September 14, 584

THE YARD WAS FULL OF HUNTSMEN AND STABLE BOYS, WAITING FOR Berto. Valrada patted her brother's restive horse. It was no more anxious than she for Berto to come and ride away from here.

Berto was late because, Valrada knew, his heart wasn't

in what the day held for him. Berto's best friend had ridden to Chelles for the king's hunt, and Berto had wanted to go with him. This year's deer hunt was more than the usual September affair. The king was sending his daughter to marry the crown prince of Spain; everyone who came for her departure ceremonies was staying for the hunt; it would be the most splendidly attended since the king's own first wedding. To have been on "The Hunt of '84" was a boast Berto could have made to his grandchildren.

Instead, he was at home trying to win a silly bet with Rikimer about whose silly bird could kill the most pigeons.

If Berto could guess how much less her heart was in what the day held for her, Valrada reflected grimly, there'd be the ax to pay. She had kept her heart secret from everyone in her family except her foster sister for more than a year now—and so, she didn't need to remind herself, she must continue to do. If she and Alarik were caught where she was about to meet him, her father could strike Alarik down with no preamble in full public view; three hundred *solidi* to the king and Alarik's brother, a few masses, and the affair would be settled.

Her own punishment—and Valrada had thought of it many times since that June day last year when the deacon had shot the doe and killed Valrada's childhood—her own punishment would be...Valrada caught her breath as Berto at last emerged from the Hall. "I was worried about that wind earlier," she called to him before he was even close enough to hear, "but it's died down. Look." She pointed back to where Poijou's far meadows thickened into forest. Above the trees' dark contour the sky's few clouds were deposited, flat and still like lumpy mattresses.

Wind would have discouraged his falcon's soaring flight
and interfered with Rikimer's goshawk not at all. "She'll
beat him."

"I should have given her more time to get used to me
before I agreed to match them. Rikimer's had his hawk a
year."

"You'll win, you'll win." Valrada walked toward the
mews, where the falcon waited, as quickly as she could
without skipping, trying to influence her brother's
reluctant pace.

He was eyeing her sideways. "I'm sorry you have to
weave this morning, Val." She saw him brace himself for
her sarcastic response to what she knew was a fib.

"Oh," she surprised him by smiling, "nobody gets
everything he wants. You wanted to go to Chelles with
Wulf."

"Yes. Well, Father's right. I'd have muffed something at
Chelles."

"He never said that. He just said——"

"'No.' You're right, Val—Father's explanations don't
run on."

Werner the mewskeeper had the falcon's block in the
warm south yard. Berto stood looking at her.

"I'll get your glove," Valrada said.

Werner stiffened like a man who sees a cockroach
scuttling across his plate. As always, Valrada pretended
not to recognize how much having a woman around his
mews offended Werner. He followed her to the mews
door, quivering for fear she would disturb one of the
hawks, or touch something on his workbench. Today she
did not torment him, as she dearly loved to do, by
inspecting everything, but emerged with the proper
gauntlet at once.

The falcon knew the glove; she stepped with disdainful confidence onto Berto's hand.

"Now go along," Valrada told him. "Go along and good luck."

The chapel in Poijou Forest was dedicated to St. Eustace, patron of the hunt, but stags came with impunity to rub their itching antlers against its corners, and grouse nested regularly under its altar. Its door had fallen to the ground and rotted long ago. Probably Poijou's current priest didn't even know the chapel was there, but the lord of Poijou's daughter did know, and she waited only until her brother's hawking party was on the road to her uncle's before setting herself onto what once had been a path to the shrine of St. Eustace.

The king's daughter required a guard for her journey to Spain, and from Poitiers to Toulouse, Alarik must serve in it. He would be gone four months.

Did he mind as much as Valrada? She didn't think so. This meeting had been her idea, and she hadn't known what to think when instead of agreeing at once he had looked reserved, thought a long time, muttered about risk. Risk to her, of course, but *she* wasn't thinking of it. Surely if he cared for her as she cared for him he would be as heedless of risk as she?

Valrada's chest ached from hurry and anxiety. Even though he'd agreed to come, she wasn't sure he would be there. He had never been to the place before; maybe she'd described it poorly; maybe he wouldn't find it. Maybe he had found it but had been unable to wait for her, Berto had stalled so long at the mews.

The shrine was little more than a shelter, with a few square holes to let in light, if any made its way through the trees. In mid-September, there was just enough for Valrada to see that she had not arrived too late. He was here and she was in his arms and he was looking into her eyes as if they would drown him. It is difficult to embrace a man in coat-of-mail wholeheartedly. Valrada managed. She was even impatient when sudden belated consideration for her made Alarik relax his arms. He never thought of his bruising sword hilt and her knees remained gripped between his. There would be a blue mark above her pelvic bone, visible proof that her body did not leave him so much in control of his mind as he imagined.

Yet the bruise would be gone long before he held her this way again. "Don't go," she whispered: "Refuse." Dark piles of wind-driven leaves rotted in every corner; the long-abandoned chapel smelled like death. There had been a pagan altar on this spot, before the chapel. God alone knew what bones lay under her feet.

"I will turn back at Toulouse," Alarik promised.

Valrada realized that he didn't need to whisper, that there was no one to hear them for miles, but surely "I'll be gone four months" was nothing to remind her in that See-you-later voice, as if he scarcely minded. "Don't hurry away from your princess just for me," she cringed to hear herself answering.

"You know very well he can't refuse," Brunehaut, Valrada's foster-sister, had admonished her, "and you won't make leaving you any less attractive by being a shrew about it." Yes, she knew, but her angry hurt feelings insisted on their own satisfaction, urging her tongue on despite her.

She regretted her words exactly as much as she had known she would, in the instant before she uttered them

face. *Dear God, let the band not come off.* The amethyst in its center made it unmistakably hers and no other's.

She recognized her brother Berto's shouts among the rest, and her cousin Rikimer's. Hawks were flown only in the open field, so why were Berto and Rikimer crashing about the forest?

They *were* coming nearer. She could imagine the shouts if they caught a glimpse of her. "What have we treed? Come down, wench! The moss is soft...." Would the men loose arrows at her if she refused to budge? She could hear the terrible rude laughter as her exposed legs groped for the branch below, and then when it was she who appeared, the silence....

The pack was so near she could hear their bells. Bells on the dogs meant they were hunting wolf or boar, but Berto hadn't gone prepared for such game. He hadn't even taken his spear.

The forest clamored as if the devil were coming. Stench began to foul the air even as high as Valrada's perch, and the boar itself plunged into sight.

Valrada's heart sank as it set its back against a thicket.

Dogs, men and horses boiled out of the woods. The men drew up sharply as they discovered the boar waiting, but the first dog was killed before the huntsmen could halt the packs. Valrada's eyes clenched as the poor creature scrabbled in its own spilled entrails trying to retreat. A second turn of the boar's head and the hound lay still.

The reined-in horses tore at the ground. The men cursed: If the boar held here they would have to dismount for the kill.

The huntsmen had leashed all the dogs. The young

ones strained, whimpering with desire. Valrada all but whimpered with them, that the huntsmen free them again, that they dislodge the boar, that the whole hunt pour off like a nightmare and free *her*.

The boar's spine bristled and its little red eyes glared at the demons who had harried it across three rivers.

Rikimer, she was surprised to see, hung back. "He's mine," Berto cried. Berto was so close that when his bangs flew up as he slid from his horse, Valrada saw the scar where she had stunned him with her crucifix years ago.

Berto's horsemen were down and following him. Each dropped to one knee and readied his spear while Berto continued to advance, alone. Sweat glued Valrada to the tree. One spear-thrust to the spine would dispatch the boar: Berto had done it before. Valrada's heart all but stopped as he approached his quarry.

Berto's spear had begun its plunge when almost simultaneously the boar's quick tusk caught him above the knee. The plunging arm never faltered—but at first contact the iron of the spear parted from its wood and fell harmlessly to the ground. Berto staggered forward, onto the slathering head. Valrada's cry was lost in a chorus of cries. The boar tossed Berto off as if he had been no more than a dipping branch's dump-load of snow. Valrada scarcely saw the huntsman leap whose knife brought the boar to its knees a bare instant after her brother's body landed. The red hair had fallen back from Berto's forehead; the red scar stared up at Valrada like the Evil Eye. For a moment she was in danger of falling.

Rikimer reached her brother first. Berto's eyes opened.

"It was your—" Valrada heard him gasp, "it——"

Rikimer's hand covered Berto's mouth. "Hush," he commanded, "you must save your strength."

The smell of warm boar's blood was driving the leashed dogs mad. Suddenly above their hysterical yapping one hound raised an eerie, upward-winding howl. Every hair on her scalp and arms pulling, Valrada recognized Berto's pet.

Berto's eyes had closed.

"God curse this day!" shouted Rikimer. "God curse this boar!" He snatched up the spear whose flaw had betrayed Berto and flung it as far as he had strength to throw.

Valrada realized that drool was running from the corner of her mouth down her stiff chin. She closed her mouth and wiped it with her hand: No one would be looking upward now.

IV

September 15, 584

FOUR YEARS AND TWO MONTHS AFTER HER THREE ELDEST BROTHERS' funeral, Valrada knelt between her mother and her foster sister Brunehaut and watched her father and his helpers set down Berto's bier. The other bearers stepped back, but Lord Eurik stood immobile.

The priest began the rites, but Valrada could see only her father.

All her life her father had walked and stood a certain way. Every footstep had asserted dominion; the thrust of his neck had defied anyone to drive him from what had become his as he set foot on it. Today he shuffled like a blind beggar.

Seeing him like that was more devastating than hearing her mother weep.

He looked as she had never seen him look: defeated. After the Brittany campaign he had been furious, contemptuous—Neustria's defeat had not been his fault; his men had been advancing when the rout of the others had swept them along and him with them, raging, but not beaten, as he was ready to tell anyone. *His* men had fought well. Valrada's face crumbled at the memory of her father pounding the table as he boasted of Berto's performance at Vannes, and Berto, across from her, glowing with pride and embarrassment.

She must go on sitting at that table, and so must her father.

She was sick with pity for him. To the Lord of Poijou, the life of a sonless man was as pointless as a barren woman's. After the staggering loss of his three eldest boys he had concentrated all the more on Berto, who had already, had always, been his favorite.

Four years ago, when plague had left him and his brother each but one son, Valrada remembered how he had stood with her uncle beside that sickeningly long line of biers, grimly erect. Her uncle's face had been washed with tears, but from her father, no public sign of weakness. Seeing him now standing before them all slump-shouldered was more than Valrada could bear.

He was blaming himself. Berto had wanted to go with Wulf Lehunsson to Chelles, for the king's hunt. Her father had said no. Had Berto gone with Wulf to Chelles, Berto would be alive.

Valrada longed to tell her father that Berto had not held this against him, but her father would not have tolerated it. That he might ever make a mistake was never to be so much as hinted at, in his own home, on his own villa.

Still less could Valrada tell him how she was blaming herself, how she had hurried Berto to his death so that she could meet a man in secret. "Now go along," she'd urged Berto, thinking only of the waiting Alarik. Had some foreboding made Berto so slow that day? "Go along," she'd told him. "Don't keep Rikimer waiting."

She looked abruptly at Rikimer, standing with the other bier-carriers: his deacon, his father. Rikimer was taller than his father, or her own—taller but sparer than any of his own late brothers had been. Who would have thought he would be the only one of her cousins the pox never touched?

As she watched, Rikimer laid one of his long hands on her father's shoulder. The pin with which he always skewered his topknot had as its handle a bleached birdskull. It stared at Valrada as Rikimer bent his head to murmur in her father's ear.

Lord Eurik's eyes stayed unfocused, but he stumbled back to let Berto's weapon be placed beside their master: Berto's sword, his throwing hatchet, the spear he only yesterday had left leaning by the hearth as he rode off to prove his falcon against Rikimer's goshawk.

The birds remained uncompared. Rikimer's goshawk had seemed unwell, Rikimer had told them all last night, so they had not dared fly it, but had chased the boar instead.

Rikimer had lent Berto a spear.

After the spear had broken and a huntsman had

dispatched the boar with a knife, Rikimer had reached Berto before the boar had rolled from its knees to its side. What was it Berto had tried to say? "It was your...idea?" "Your...spear?" "Your...fault?" The priest was laying a cross on Berto's chest. Beside Valrada, her mother shook with sobs. Valrada put one arm protectively around her shoulders. She ought to have arranged that her mother kneel between herself and Brunehaut, she thought sadly. In the past she had been jealous that Brunehaut always seemed better at comforting Lady Chrona, but today she urgently wanted her mother to get any comfort she could get. Lady Chrona was pale, pale as the ashes she had smeared in her hair, and her shoulders under Valrada's arm felt insubstantial as ashes.

The chief groom deposited the severed head of Berto's horse at Berto's feet and turned back, wet-faced. His grief would be at least half for the horse, but Valrada was sure that he and all Poijou's people did sincerely mourn her brother. They had been counting on him to be their next lord. Rikimer was the kind who gave his flocks the freedom of his tenants' grainfields, telling his herdsmen to beat any farmer who dared drive the beasts out. Now between Poijou's farmers and Rikimer stood only Berto's father, and Rikimer's. Both were past forty.

Rikimer's rage had been a show.

Valrada could swear it.

Why was this only now coming to her? Rikimer's anger was freezing, not raving. Her own blood was suddenly gelid as one more time her mind replayed the scene the memory of which, she thought, was surely going to drive her mad.

She ought to have looked for that spear. Why hadn't

she realized at once that as soon as the men had retreated out of hearing, she ought to have looked for this spear that had parted so easily from its head?

The priest began his invocation. Lady Chrona's hands covered her eyes; tears streamed through the swollen-knuckled fingers. Valrada stared at Rikimer, suddenly dry-eyed.

V

September 17, 584

TWO DAYS AFTER BERTO'S FUNERAL, WEAVING RESUMED AT Poijou Hall. Valrada threw her shuttle back and forth, conscious each time of Alarik's ring. Brunehaut had promised to say that she had given it to Valrada, should anyone notice it. Lord Eurik hadn't emerged from his office in two days, and Lady Chrona had tottered from the graveyard to her bed, where she still lay, scarcely opening her eyes to accept water. However, neither would remain blind forever—or so Valrada urgently told herself. If people died of grief, surely they all would have died four years ago.

At the loom next to Valrada, Brunehaut shuttled mechanically. Was she thinking of Berto, or of her parents? Brunehaut had come to Poijou as the orphan of the same plague that had carried off all Valrada's brothers but Berto. Valrada bit her cheek: She must *not* think of Berto; she would cry in front of the weaving women.

Brunehaut's face was admirably stoic—but would she be sitting there if she had seen what Valrada had seen? Valrada couldn't ask her. She could confide in no one except Alarik, which until January meant no one. And in January? How could she have let her last words to Alarik be sharp? He had ignored them, he had kissed her, but when he thought about it—and he would have months to think about it before he saw her again—how many other times when she had blurted out something sarcastic would he remember? Would they become what he mostly remembered? "Your habit of speaking before you analyze causes grief to yourself as well as to others," her mother was always preaching at her.

Something else her mother was always claiming was less certain but at the moment more comfort. "Love forgives everything." Valrada had never liked to hear that, always seeming to be the injured party when her mother said it to her, but now she thought it might help if her mother were right. Her arms tingled as she remembered Alarik's words when he had given her his ring.

The ring was loose. Its stone was a signet, a stag springing out of carnelian, and Valrada realized that Alarik had chosen it for her despite its size because a deer had first brought them together. She said a prayer for Berto, who had been with them that June day, alive and with them.

She must not let her thoughts stray to Berto. Three days ago, the idea that any subject might move her to tears more quickly than Alarik, who was leaving her, would have made her laugh: a bitter laugh, but a laugh. Could anything make anyone on Poijou laugh now, ever? Her mother's face was a stranger's, pillowed on her long, ash-streaked hair, still unbraided like a maiden's from the burial: She lacked even the strength to sit up and have it redone. Valrada went to bed with a pain below her ribs, and as she opened her eyes in the morning she felt it there still, just waiting for her to wake up enough to remember why. *She must think of Alarik.*

When she had heard the horse coming that June day she had known whose it would be. Suddenly she had been unable to watch him walk toward her. The little chestnut-colored hearts that hung from the quaking grass had trembled on their threads. The fawn, warm on her lap, suddenly had felt enormous.

He had sat down beside her.

He had said very little; her own tongue, as always, had run away. "I doubt if my cousin's horse could bear your weight." He'd looked her in the eye at that; she had felt her cheeks heat. The bird's full-throated song had given her space to keep her face turned away.

He had lifted her onto her horse as if she were too fine to touch. Berto, if he helped her at all, grabbed her around the calves and shoved, grunting. Alarik had lifted her as if she were weightless.

She'd ridden out of the forest ahead of him, high above the earth.

By the time the quaking grass bloomed again, the deer had left the pen behind Alarik's cottage—she hoped, to find its kind.

Fleet, as they'd named their foundling, had grown in that one year hopelessly unrestrainable, her love for Alarik barely less so.

Valrada shuttled in a sort of trance; Alarik's ring with its vaulting stag flashed back and forth. The ring was so loose, Valrada was likely to lose it as she'd lost Fleet.

She would bind the ring with reed until it would rest. Alarik was like the real Fleet; to bind him until he would rest wouldn't be so easy.

"Why," she had demanded, "do you let your brother keep *all* your father's freehold? It isn't a virtue, to let yourself be cheated! Your father never meant to disinherit you!" If he loved her, the unspoken charge crackled the long, too long, distance between them, he would demand his inheritance and at least ask her father, at least try.

Alarik had lifted and dropped his shoulders, not so much shrugging off the accusation as shifting its weight to a sensible position. Alarik was always sensible; there were times when Valrada could have scratched him. "My half wouldn't keep soup in our bowls. My brother can just maintain himself in armor with the whole. It's easier for me to commend myself to your father than for my brother, with a wife and three children."

"You are to have no children because your brother's wife has three?"

"I can have a dozen sons—by some freeholder's daughter. If children is all you want me to have, I can marry today." He had actually laughed at her.

She had been devastated. Did he mind their predicament less than she? She felt hollow with shock and humiliation.

She had marched home, a picture of Alarik, with his dowryless bride and their dozen barefoot sons, filling her mind. She had thought herself unfortunate beyond any justification God could offer. Yet Berto had been alive, then.

Domnola the Breton slave stood in the weaving room doorway. "Lord Eurik asks to see you, my lady."

Valrada's father hadn't left his office since Berto's funeral. Valrada opened its door and hesitated. Her father's mastiff rubbed its greasy head against her skirt, and her father hitched his chair around to face her.

His brows were knit, the red birthmark he habitually rubbed for luck puckered out. Not for the first time the mark reminded Valrada of Berto's scar, the one she'd given him, and she winced. Lord Eurik cleared his throat.

Rikimer and his father could pay a good bridal price. The Morning Gift* Rikimer presented his wife would be substantial.

Valrada groped backward for the wall. Her father seemed sober. Marry Rikimer? She felt the blood rush to her head. She knew what her father thought of her cousin; he didn't like Rikimer—yet she was to marry Rikimer? The mastiff was on its feet before she'd said three words. "Rikimer's sons will all burn in hell!" The wind roared in her ears and she stopped to take a deep breath before saying more, more slowly, at least at first. "He makes his living robbing St. Martin's pilgrims. Is that the trade you want for your grandsons? Do you want your grandsons in that trade?"

"All pilgrims get robbed," said Eurik. "Better by our kin than by the church. The Bishop of Tours is no friend to Poitou," he added. "Your cousin shares what he takes with our own priests, here."

"Oh, yes, he steals a hog and gives God the feet."

Eurik felt the back of his neck prickle. He'd never loosed his temper on his daughter. She'd never crossed him. "Don't," he let the advice come from low in his throat,

---

*The Morning Gift was the settlement a Frankish groom made on his bride the second day of their marriage to compensate her for the virginity she had surrendered to him the night before.

"bite a tame dog on the lip, girl." The mastiff began butting insistently at his thigh; he ignored it.

She stared at him. He couldn't mean this marriage; God could not treat her so. Her sins had not been that great. She was as helpless as a netted fish. To plead love for Alarik, a man she wasn't even supposed to befriend, would be like running from a snake into a bear's cave. Valrada's fingers dug for her wits. Had Rikimer tampered with the spear, or not? If she accused him and her father believed her, the count would order trial by combat. Her father would have to fight Rikimer, who if he were innocent, would win. She would sit watching while her cousin killed her father, and then, for her false accusation, they would burn her.

The bird under her ribs flew about desperately seeking a way out, bruising itself headlong against first one wall, then another, baffled at every corner, and at last fluttered helplessly in a numbed heap. "Lord—I cannot—" she stammered. "*Father*," she threw herself on her knees. "I would rather be a nun; let me take the veil!"

His forehead flushed red as a thresher's, the mark only a shadow on it. (How Berto's had stared at her from his blood-drained face!) "You're too quick to drop to the rushes to make a nun, wench!"

This was for her sins: She had loved Alarik and God had sent her to the forest to see a spear fail and never know if Rikimer, or the devil, had spoiled a good lance— to tempt her to defy her father.

"You'll marry your cousin. Let's have no more drivel about convents."

Valrada knew what came next. He would lock her in her room, and anyone helping her escape would die for it. In the convent of Radegonda of Poitiers she would be safe, but Alarik, who might have spirited her there, was leagues away. January, he'd said. "Then let me," she whispered, "wait until spring."

"St. Denis's Day," Eurik enjoyed answering. The church wouldn't perform a wedding with less warning than that date gave. He beat on the desk with both fists for a servant.

Valrada jumped up from the floor as if her knees were scorched. "It will kill me if you marry me to Rikimer!" she screamed. "And if I curse you as I die, it will be your sin as well as mine!"

"Out!" his arm shook as it pointed. "Out!"

She rushed to her room rather than be taken.

VI

Same day

THUDDING HOOFS IN THE COURTYARD BELOW BROUGHT VALRADA to her window. Her cousin Rikimer and his deacon were dismounting. She stared down at her cousin's flaxen knot and the deacon's tonsure and her mouth twisted with the impulse to spit. She would have liked to empty her chamber pot on the two of them, but it was already empty. (She had dumped slops on Berto once. Her father had taken the flat of his sword to her.) She settled for spit, and it missed both men; tears scalded her eyes.

The two riders passed into Poijou Hall.

Valrada had always heard that cranes followed a

murderer, but nothing flew across the sky but a flock of noisy crows. Maybe, like a scavenging crow, Rikimer in inheriting Poijou would only be feeding on Berto's death, but hadn't made the kill himself. If she only could know. . . .

Marry Rikimer! Surely he would refuse! What he craved was land, and what would he get with Valrada that he wouldn't get without her, just by waiting? He was his father's only heir, and his father's and her father's villas would be united anyhow, once her father died. All Rikimer would lose by refusing her was her dowry, and if he married the daughter of someone as rich as her father, then that girl's dowry would be as good as Valrada's—and he wouldn't have to live with the sister of a man he'd murdered. Valrada flung herself across her bed.

She was up again in a moment as the sound of more horses clattered up from the courtyard. She leaped to her window just in time to see her uncle and Lehun of Claigne's eldest son running—*running*—into Poijou Hall.

What was Wulf Lehunsson doing here? She hoped Brunehaut would come, for God's sake, and tell her what was going on. Wulf was supposed to be at Chelles, two hundred miles away.

The servant at Valrada's door had orders from Lord Eurik to let Lady Brunehaut enter and talk some sense into his daughter.

Valrada whirled from the window. Seeing Brunehaut, she began to talk at once, too fast for Brunehaut to comprehend more than half.

"You must make up with your father at once,"

Brunehaut interrupted, "or it will be too late. Your cousin leaves for Paris within the week. The king has been assassinated."

Valrada sank onto her bed. "The king?"

"It was at Chelles; he was dismounting from the hunt. Wulf saw it. Someone just ran up and stabbed him."

"How could...? Who...?"

"No one knows. It was twilight, Wulf says, and the man ran back into the crowd before anyone really got a look at him. Mobs of strangers gather for those hunts.

"The queen fled with the princeling right away to Paris Cathedral, Wulf says. Nobody knows who might be next."

"Has someone seized the throne?" Valrada's voice came out a whisper.

Brunehaut shook her head. "Paris was quiet when Wulf left—which was four days ago, of course. But the Austrasian army is marching doubletime to get there, and so are the Burgundians. Gontram of Burgundy vows he's only coming to protect his brother's son from the Austrasians, but—"

"So Wulf and Rikimer are going. What about my father and uncle?"

"Your father says his men will march on the Count of Poitiers' orders, and your uncle——"

"Agrees with him; always." The young men with no lands would join whichever army looked stronger; the men who had villas already would wait and declare for the victor when the fight was settled. Of course Rikimer was going. Wulf would probably go with him. Berto would have, too. And Alarik?

"Your father is wild. Your cousin Rikimer heard you

were begging to become a nun and says he won't come between any girl and the convent. Your father even offered to waive your Morning Gift, but Rikimer refuses to force himself on you. You have just three days, Valrada, if you don't want to spend the winter in this room!"

"So you'd like to see me betrothed to Rikimer."

Brunehaut sat down. "Not to obey your father is a sin. Your cousin won't be a bad husband. Don't——"

"——jump to conclusions. Just once you could get through a lecture to me without that."

Brunehaut sighed. "I brought our embroidering. Using our hands will quiet our stomachs and help us think." She held out Valrada's hoop.

Valrada turned her face like a nausea victim offered fatback.

Through the corner of her eye she saw Brunehaut's needle begin to stitch.

"You may even learn to love Rikimer. If you're wise, and never see Alarik, that love will fade."

That love would never fade.

Brunehaut breathed slowly as a rock; the lily on her cloth grew. She wasn't so granitic when *she* had troubles. Valrada well remembered how Brunehaut had sobbed her first day at Poijou, and the next, and the next.

Maybe Rikimer would be killed fighting the Austrasians; was it a sin to hope so? Not, obviously, if he was Berto's murderer. Valrada's mind had gone over the scene so often she was no longer even sure what she had seen and what imagined later, let alone what any of it meant. What would Brunehaut think?

Brunehaut had never been up a tree in her life, neither

figuratively nor truly. Brunehaut never did anything she wasn't supposed to do, went anywhere she wasn't supposed to go. She would be neither understanding nor helpful. No, the only one Valrada could talk to was Alarik.

Alarik must return from Toulouse before Rikimer returned from Paris, must simply return and take her away.

Even if Alarik could come for her, where could he take her? Years before, Valrada shuddered at the memory, two of her father's slaves had married against his will and taken refuge in a church. The priest would not give them up and Lord Eurik had gone to the bishop and demanded their return. "You cannot take these two from God's church," the bishop had replied, "unless you pledge to honor their union." Eurik had placed his hands on the altar and sworn that the slaves should not be parted.

He had buried them alive, together.

VII

Same day

"BUT SURELY," RIKIMER ANSWERED HIS UNCLE, "YOU COULDN'T want your daughter marrying a man already horsed for combat. Should my poor cousin receive widowhood for her Morning Gift?" The deacon looked solemn.

"This war talk is one more reason for the girl to marry at once." Eurik leaned forward. "Poijou will be my grandson's. I haven't worked my arse off keeping it together all these years for anybody else."

"*He heapeth up riches, and knoweth not who shall gather them,*" the deacon sighed.

Lord Eurik of Poijou was not accustomed to interruptions, but he ignored the deacon this time, to show contempt. "My wife fails daily since our son's death; it's plain she'll not survive her grief."

Uncle and nephew looked at each other steadily for a moment, then Rikimer shrugged and turned away.

"My lady is weaker every day," Eurik reproved Greek Nicolaus, Poijou's doctor. "She has too much blood: The labor to pump it is exhausting her heart. She should be cupped."

The Greek bled Lady Chrona once each day for three days.

With his nephew's departure for Paris, Lord Eurik ceased to care whether Valrada sprouted wings like the harpy he considered her and flew back and forth over his Hall screaming and defecating, or sat in her bedroom and played with her toes. Valrada was permitted to leave her room and go with the rest of Poijou to the graveyard.

They had come for her too late for her to say good-bye. Nicolaus the doctor had been with her mother, but he had thought Lady Chrona was only dropping off to sleep. Before he could move from her bed to the door to send for Lord Eurik, she was gone.

Back at the Hall, Valrada returned straight to her room without even trying to learn whether her father still required it, too numb to speak. When Claudia brought her lunch soup, Valrada was standing at her window, chin on the heels of her hands. When Claudia returned to take away the dish, nothing had changed except the sky, which was somewhat cloudier, and the soup, which was cold.

Steel-blue swallows swooped and darted over the court. Sometimes when a school of gnats hovered like minnows in front of Valrada's window, a gape-mouthed bird would appear to be flying straight at her. The bird would hurtle so close Valrada could see the bristles on its cheeks, then with a flash of wings it would turn, swoop, rise, turn again, until insects crammed its mouth. Yet despite the swallows' pitiless appetites, whenever a cloud passed over the sun, they seemed to be in mourning.

Behind Valrada her door opened. Claudia had returned with two folding chairs and another of Lady Chrona's women, carrying sewing. So, Valrada thought indifferently, she was still not to be unguarded.

The swallows were gathering to leave Poijou; they squeaked and twittered. *Yea, the stork in the heaven knoweth her appointed times, and the turtle and the crane and the swallow observe the time of their going.* Had her mother known her appointed time? Valrada closed her eyes.

"All sunshine makes a desert," her mother had reminded her often. Enough salt tears would make one, too, Valrada thought bitterly.

When at length she took her hands away from her eyes, there was not one swallow in the court. She would have noticed a sudden silence—her weeping had been soundless—but the twittering had continued. Slowly, she realized it was from the women behind her. As soon as she had made the effort to understand their Latin chatter, she regretted it.

"I wouldn't say our old master grieves for his wife as he grieves for our young master, would you?" Claudia was saying.

Valrada froze. The women didn't realize how well she spoke their tongue.

The old one tittered. "He'll replace both, you'll see. Maybe he has somebody in mind already—maybe already four days ago . . ."

Valrada snatched up the nearest object and hurled it at the old woman's head. "Get out!" she screamed. The missile turned out to be the box in which Valrada's headband lay at night; fortunately, its lid flew open and spoiled its aim. It thudded onto the rushes just past Claudia, who dropped her needle and froze.

"Leave," Valrada repeated coldly. If father had ordered that she was not to be alone, they could sit in the hall. *How* could they say such things? Their mistress had been the gentlest, the kindest, had *freed* Claudia. . . .

Curtseying, the older witch shuffled for the door. Claudia risked pausing to search for her needle among the rushes. "That too," Valrada pointed to the box. Claudia picked it up as if it were hot, dropped it on the seat of the nearest chair, and fled.

Brunehaut had vowed to spend the afternoon on her knees in the oratory, for her foster mother's sake, but at Claudia's report she rose quickly. It was she who had sent Claudia and the old woman to Valrada's room, because Valrada's eyes, as the bearers had laid her mother facing east, had been frightening.

As Brunehaut reached the foot of the stairs leading to the second floor, she looked up and saw Lord Eurik coming. The air closed in on her and out again, leaving her weak. Had he been with Valrada?

Lord Eurik's tramp, always emphatic, proceeded down the hall toward the stair head as if each step were an assertion never to be retracted.

Brunehaut forced her own suddenly leaden feet to keep the same pace as before she'd seen him.

Eurik blocked her path. "You are well, girl?" he asked. "You feel quite well today?"

Brunehaut's apprehension softened. Her foster father seldom inquired after anyone's health. Perhaps he was touched by his wife's death more than anyone had believed. The back of his hand scrubbed at his forehead; Brunehaut felt a rush of sympathy.

"When your father left you to my care," Eurik cut off her answer, "I promised to marry you to a good husband. What if I can't think of any better than myself?"

As Brunehaut gasped, Eurik's frown deepened. "Because I can't. The priest will marry us Monday." He stepped past and left her leaning there against the wall, staring after him.

The mourning servants slipped out of his path like shadows as he stamped through the forehall. Servants were richer than lords—Eurik kicked the front door open. Mourning was a luxury. They could afford it; he could not.

Eurik strode toward the stables. He had no time to send away for somebody. (His damned nephew was counting on that.) Buying a wife took time, and Eurik didn't know how many days were left before he would have to take sides between Gontram and Austrasia. He had given the priest sixty *solidi* to celebrate masses for Lady Chrona's soul, and the priest had agreed to dispense with the reading of banns for the new marriage. If the wench was any good he would have a new son by midsummer. Rikimer could piss up the wind.

VIII

Late September 584

THE RING, THE KISS, AND THE SHOE WERE GIVEN, BUT THERE was no wedding feast. All the potential guests were in mourning.

The new Lady of Poijou went straight from the oratory to her room, her own old room. She did not dare remove the ring, but she scrubbed her mouth where he had kissed her and she placed his shoe in the fireplace. She didn't light the fire because she wanted him to see his shoe on it first.

Her arms trembled to comb out her hair. She knew now how a man felt when his enemies shaved his head. She had felt naked from the moment Claudia had begun braiding.

When she had it all unbound she sat rubbing her scalp, her neck bent forward, her hair falling down over her knees, curtaining her from everything.

She cringed to remember the times she had fantasied how proud she would feel when her hair was finally braided for marriage.

There was no thought she could light on that didn't scorch her.

Work and prayer, her mother had said, would see man through every trial. Brunehaut picked up her distaff and made the spindle dance. As she twisted the thread she whispered a Hail Mary, and when this didn't quite smother her thoughts, she tried saying the next one louder.

It was not a success.

Her door had no bolt. Someone was coming down the hall—but the steps were a woman's. Brunehaut crossed the room swiftly and lay down on her bed, her face away from the doorway; when the knock came she stiffened. The door opened softly. "Brunehaut?" Brunehaut lay rigid. Valrada might or might not believe she was sleeping, but she did go away.

Brunehaut sat up. The crucifix that had hung above Lady Chrona's bed lay on Brunehaut's pillow. Brunehaut had quietly possessed herself of it yesterday. She snatched up her flax and began another Hail Mary.

To put a bench across the door would be to acknowledge Lord Eurik's existence, would be to acknowledge that she was conscious of what was being done to her.

Neither Lord Eurik's wife nor his daughter appeared for supper. He would tolerate this tonight, but not again. He looked up and down the table for someone to savage, but every neck was pulled well into its shell.

He stopped drinking the minute he finished eating.

He entered the girl's room without knocking. She was already in bed. She lay on her back with something which he thought for a second was a knife clasped in her hands on her chest. Then he saw it was the crucifix which had hung above his and Lady Chrona's bed for twenty years. He took hold of it with one hand and the bedcover with the other, throwing the one against the wall and the other to the foot of the bed. She didn't open her eyes or move. She didn't know it, but she should be glad her trick hadn't worked. If it had spoiled him, he would have beaten her. And that would probably have restored him, so she would have gotten it anyway. "You know how it's done?" he asked. She gave no sign of life. "It won't take long and then I'll leave you."

He held himself up with his elbows and never touched her anywhere else.

She began to throw up almost before he was out of the room. She managed to get it all on the rushes, but when she had finished she threw the sheet and her nightgown onto the laid fire and lit it before she even added the soiled rushes. She kept her teeth clenched to keep her crying as quiet as possible. When she began to clean her legs, she threw up again. She spent the night gagging and washing and prodding the fire.

IX

November 10, 584

THE SKY WAS DOVE-GRAY WHEN CLAUDIA CAME TO WAKEN Valrada, with the rose of the dove's throat where the sun would soon rise. Valrada set her teeth, counted three, and threw back her sheepskin. It was like diving into an icy well. She splashed her face with water Claudia had broken ice to draw, blinked, shuddered, wiped her face, and looked twice at Claudia.

The girl had been crying. Valrada's glance went at once to Claudia's arm. The bracelet still glinted there. Valrada felt foolish for being glad. Normally, she assured herself, she wouldn't have stooped to interest in a servant's amours (where but from a lover would this Roman girl get a gold bracelet?), but her mind was desperate for distraction from its relentless diet of worry and sorrow.

The one mercy she'd been able to grant herself—

daydreams born when Alarik first had been assigned to the princess's escort—had died with the king. Before his murder, Valrada had found relief imagining a score of mischances. Ambushes, rabid wolves, floods, had afflicted the princess's caravan in Valrada's waking dreams, each crisis settled more valiantly than the last, always by Alarik. On his hero's return the king would reward him with such lands that Valrada's father himself would suggest her to Alarik as a match. These dreams had spilled away with the king's blood.

"I want my hair combed," she told Claudia.

Her mother had never permitted hair-combing on Sunday. Her mother: Valrada pressed her fist against her mouth.

Her mother had never permitted hair-combing on Sunday, but Valrada was determined to keep Claudia long enough to hear about the night's vigil. The summons had come. The infant prince was to be baptized and raised on the shield before Christmas: The Neustrian oathman who didn't ride for Paris now was declaring for Childebert of Austrasia. "What were the omens last night?"

"It's said that a glittering star was seen to shine in the center of the moon, *mea Domina*. The priests say the star is our princeling, smaller but brighter than the moon, his uncle of Burgundy. But the moon was truly behind the star, so it's said King Gontram's heart is open when he declares he will protect our prince from the Austrasians, and see him crowned king of Neustria. Your father and your uncle take their men to Paris."

Valrada could hear the choke in Claudia's voice as she said "to Paris." So that was it. Well, Claudia's beloved, whoever he was, would be back as soon as Alarik, so why should Valrada feel sorry for Claudia? Berto would never be back.

And Rikimer? She must think about something else.

Maybe with Lord Eurik gone, Valrada brooded, Brunehaut would talk to her again. In the month and a half since Claudia had fettered Brunehaut's hair in braids, Brunehaut hadn't once looked Valrada in the face. Sometimes Valrada almost wished she were still confined to her room, the Hall was so strange now, so painfully changed.

Lover, brother, mother, and friend, all gone in one season. The year of the plague had seemed like the end of happiness: What joy would she go back to what she had then possessed!

"There were a multitude of stars very near the moon, *mea Domina,* and the priests are studying whether these are the loyal oathmen, gathered to raise His Infant Highness Clotar on the shield, or his enemies, the army of Austrasia." Claudia broke off and knelt to get Valrada's mantle from its chest. Valrada saw her furtively raise one shoulder to wipe at a tear. "Oh, *mea Domina,*" Claudia sobbed, "my little sister has been raped."

Valrada hadn't been aware that Claudia had a sister. "Was it a Frank or a Roman? Was it one of my father's men? Was it a free man?"

Claudia continued to weep. "She won't name the man, *mea Domina.*"

So it was that kind of rape. "Is your father beating her?" No doubt Claudia wanted Valrada to coax Brunehaut to give the sister duties where the father couldn't reach her.

Claudia's tears ceased abruptly. "I—we have no parents."

Valrada considered this. "Then what," she asked at last, "is the matter?"

Claudia's dark eyes seemed to focus on her sandals. "My sister is afraid to make confession. She's sure the priest will say it's a sin to be raped, and make her stand in church in goat skins and tell everyone of her wickedness before she may eat holy bread again. But without the bread she will go to hell! *Mea Domina,* what is the church's penalty for being raped?"

"There is none. But your sister," Valrada thought she'd better point out, "can't run to the priest and say she was raped two months ago: A priest has to be almost as intelligent as other people."

Claudia didn't look up.

"Tell your sister to confess," Valrada said gently. "Fornication is a mortal sin and if she doesn't repent and receive absolution she will burn forever. Besides, perhaps the priest can get the man to marry her. And now, come; being late to mass is a sin, too."

Same day

EARLY ON THE TENTH AFTERNOON OF NOVEMBER, THE PRINCESS OF Neustria's forward guard surmounted the hill which put them in view of the red-walled ducal city of Toulouse. Fifty miles beyond, their snows just visible, glimmered the white-peaked Pyrenees, and Spain.

From the princess and her hand-picked escort back through the pack camels and ox-drawn wagons to their rear guard was a long way. Behind the fiftieth and final wagon, Erman of Niort swore and spat. "Somebody up there's hanging back again."

Alarik nodded. The drivers had orders not to let their wagons string out, but an outlaw attack was only a possibility, whereas the white dust swirling from each driver's predecessor was unarguably real. All day the oathmen had had to ride herd up and down the caravan, cursing and threatening.

"Just trot up till you find the man that's lagging and break your spear across his back," Lord Erman said.

Alarik rode along the caravan shouting at each driver to close up. Grit squeaked between his teeth. Where the road rose steeply, the wagons were taking the hill one at a time. Alarik scowled at the waiting team: The lead ox had a fresh scrape. It would soon be caked white, like the poor beast's nostrils. The wagon was loaded with gold plate and dresses, as if there were nothing to eat on or wear in Spain. Alarik trotted grimly on, but at the top of the hill he stopped and for a moment felt his anger lift. Spread out for incalculable miles before him lay the blue-gray plain of Toulouse.

Also before him was the culprit Lord Erman had sent him to whack. Beside a stream that branched off from the road below, the four-wheeled *rheda* and its escort had halted. From Alarik's height the bees embroidered on the *rheda*'s curtains were only golden spots, but the young woman who stood beside it couldn't be mistaken for any other. There'd be no whackings, then, though Alarik considered that several would have done her good.

From behind Alarik a rider trotted up out of the dust. "So," the newcomer regarded the halted *rheda.* "Lord Erman sent me after you; he was afraid you'd never hit an ox hard enough. He didn't say anything about bitches."

Alarik was used to Luther. Two months ago the same summons that had plunged Alarik into gloom had elated Luther of the Bourre. His pride at being singled out had received its first check when he learned that almost all the dukes had left the princess's caravan before he even joined it. By prearrangement, these high and mighties had turned around at Poitiers and trotted back to Chelles and the king's autumn hunt, which Luther was too poor to attend.

Luther equally resented the few nobles who did remain, for they were numerous enough that no one of his rank ever got close to the princess. He was ashamed for the others at the caravan's rear to see him there, and made bitter, self-deprecatory remarks to them about his grandfather (who'd never sat a horse in his life) and his father (who'd been a miller). He never reflected that no one who was there to hear these remarks, which he did not succeed in passing off as jokes, was stationed any closer to the princess than he.

"Look," Luther pointed, "one of the ineffables is coming back." A horseman had detached himself from the honor guard and was riding toward the hill, shouting at the camel and wagon drivers as he reached them. The rest of the *rheda's* escort had all dismounted and stood talking to the princess and her women. The caravan was rumbling to a halt and the lead wagon seemed to be pulling off onto the grass. "What in the name of God are they up to down there?"

"That's Lord Uldin coming," Alarik said, "probably to tell us."

Erman of Niort's brother Uldin clattered up the hill and saluted. "We're camping here for the night."

"Night?" Alarik didn't believe him, but already down by the stream the princess's tent was going up.

"Here," said Lord Uldin, "for the night." He rode on.

"Holy St. Hilary!" Luther exploded. "Secret as the moon at midnight, that's how I like my camps!"

"You'd think nothing ever came out of these hills after dark to prey but owls," Alarik muttered. "I was congratulating us we'd be well past them come dusk."

The road from the flimsy tent to the tower-girdled city ran straight and wide. "Would you say," Luther asked casually, "it was nine leagues?"

"Or eight."

"Would you say we could be there by nightfall?"

"Or sooner."

"Would you say that her royalest of majesties anticipates an end to a different lord in her tent every night, once the Bishop of Toulouse gets hold of her?"

Alarik smiled. "Would you say," he nodded toward the mountains ranked behind the ducal city like great white-sailed warships, "that you can understand why our grandsires turned back after capturing Toulouse?"

Luther laughed. "I intend to turn back there myself."

"And I." Watching the next wagon pull laboriously off the road, Alarik realized that the muscles in the back of his neck had tightened. If the princess could have spared her ox-drawn loot she could have been safe in Toledo by now, instead of a sitting duck on this pond-flat plain, and he could have been on his way home. The comparison of the girl he'd left with the woman he served drew Alarik's mouth in as if he had washed it with tannin.

"Of course *my* great-grandfather *walked* back," Luther said: "All three hundred miles."

"And mine." It hadn't been so many.

"Of course he wasn't weighted down with anything so expensive as chain mail. He armored his chest with hair. His own hair," Luther added, lest Alarik think his great-grandfather had owned a goatskin.

"Maybe we should ride back before Lord Erman kills his brother," Alarik suggested.

"Why? There are too damned many lords." The picture of Lord Erman's rage at Lord Uldin's orders cheered Luther and he turned his horse after Alarik's.

XI

Same day

THE LAST WAGON WAS IN THE CIRCLE. "I MEAN TO LOOK AROUND a bit," Alarik said.

Luther grimaced and wiped his forehead. "Right."

Together Alarik and Luther rode in and around the hills commanding the ill-chosen campsite for an hour without finding anything more suspicious than a broken pot, which could have been there a month. "We might as well turn back," Luther said.

Alarik looked searchingly at the next ridge and turned Storm back toward the plain.

Near the outskirts of the pines they stopped to gather

firewood. Alarik took off his cloak and tied its corners together for a kindling bag. The sun glistened on the pine needles as he stuffed them in. It was criminal to make camp with the sun so high; wasteful and dangerous. Light caught a stalk of purple flowers hanging bell-like over a clutter of rocks. Alarik paused. Flowers in November.... This morning he'd seen peasants pruning their vines. On Poijou he wouldn't dare do that before March. A breeze shook the purple bells and suddenly Alarik's forehead broke into a sweat.

On the largest rock, a ruff of hair had lifted in the breeze. At Alarik's exclamation, the "rock" lifted its face, a wise little fox face with what looked like a scar on one cheek. Alarik let his armload slide—the fox was gone before it landed. He whirled: Luther was looking at him. "Did you see that?"

"What?"

"Let's get back to camp."

He hadn't dreamed of that vixen in a long time; he hadn't seen her in years.

He felt sick.

He had imagined the scar, he told himself. He had seen the rock uncurl and run away on fox legs, but the scar he had imagined.

The first dream the vixen had sent him had come his tenth summer, soon after he had gazed at her in his brother's trap, her pupils shrunk to slits with fear and rage.

Twice that week a fox had made off with one of his mother's chickens, and Alarik was told to find its earth and kill it.

He had begun conscientiously. The stream through his father's woods had a high slope for its south bank—

sunny, easy to dig, just the place for a fox den. Alarik went so quietly that a turtle family, sunning themselves on a log across the stream, never moved until his shadow fell on them. When their five instantaneous *plops* had smoothed into a single final circular ripple, the soft cooing of wood pigeons was the loudest sound. Then from a distance he heard a cuckoo's call.

He never heard the mate's answer. A row blazed up somewhere between him and it that sounded like his mother when he ripped his shirt. Crows, he deduced, had found a roosting owl; he scrambled up the stream bank and ran to see.

The crows were denouncing not a branch but a thicket. Crouched within was a fox, a freshly killed rabbit between its jaws. Alarik grabbed for his hatchet.

The fox was quicker. The rabbit was abandoned to the triumphant crows and the fox gone before Alarik could throw. Alarik resumed his search encouraged, because chances were the fox had been taking that rabbit to cubs. Their nest must be near.

By afternoon he found the rocky opening on a little plateau of the stream bank. In front of the burrow the litter of bones, the sprinkling of feathers (those of his mother's missing hens clamorous among them), told him "fox" unmistakably. He climbed a downwind tree and waited, throwing hatchet in hand.

When the fox came, Alarik made a mistake which ended by costing him a beating, and worse, a nightmare that, taking all the guises of a cloud, visited him at patternless intervals the rest of his life. He waited to see what the fox would do.

The fox dropped its kill, a squirrel, and coughed twice. In a moment a sharp nose poked warily out of the opening in the bank, followed by the sharp eyes and ears of the vixen. Sight of the squirrel lifted the ruddy hair at the base of her delicate head. She tore at the corpse, ripping and gulping. Still Alarik's hand didn't move. He was almost positive he had seen the dark behind the den door stir.

When the vixen had done for the bulk of the carcass, she also coughed. Instantly, three puppy faces peered out of the den. The cubs first looked all around with a caution that was comical, it was so obviously learned and not felt. Then they rushed to investigate what had so engrossed their mother.

The fox stretched himself out facing his family; the vixen lay down beside him and together they watched their offspring pull, shake, and snarl at the dead squirrel. The fox's pride in his kill, his mate's in their cubs, was so obvious that Alarik began to feel reservations.

Compared to the clean-limbed, cunning foxes, his mother's louse-infested, witless chickens were unengaging. Alarik could sit down nowhere in the yard where they scurried about scratching and splatting. He wished the foxes would eat more of them. He was given to bad dreams, and one of the worst featured the obscenity of one chicken's reaction to another's hurt. Let any hen show the smallest shine of blood, and the others were on her like piglets on a fallen sow. When that happened his mother didn't demand that he wring the neck of every murderess in the yard, so why did she expect him to kill this beautiful pair who lay now side by side, their pink tongues grooming one another with a solicitude as different from the crazed hens' beaking as the frisking cubs were from the rotten eggs Alarik sometimes knelt on by distinct mistake? Alarik sat motionless on his branch until some other disturbance sent the foxes into hiding. Then he went home to supper and reported defeat.

He should have made it obvious to the foxes that their haven was discovered. They would have moved at once.

His mother would churn her own butter next morning if Alarik continued his search—and her own orders had been to look for that den and not stop till it was scotched. She eyed Alarik suspiciously, knowing that he loved loafing in the woods infinitely better than plunging her churn dasher, and Alarik looked at his bowl, knowing he was even guiltier than she thought.

His brother was worse. He didn't know why he hadn't thought of it before, he said: He would set his rabbit trap where the fox would pass on its way to the hen roost. "That leaves his vix, but if taking him doesn't teach her to stay out of our yard, we'll set it again and take her too." The bright-eyed, furry cubs could be counted on to starve.

Alarik tried to hope. His brother's trap wasn't the costly kind that grabbed an animal by its leg. His contraption was fine for rabbits: When one entered it for the cabbage leaves left inside, its gate crashed down. In the morning the trapper would lift the gate, reach in for the terror-frozen rabbit and wring its neck. Alarik would have liked to see his brother try that with his fox.

"I'll tie a rope to the trap before I set it," his brother said thoughtfully. "Once the fox is in there I'll hang it in the river till the bubbles stop coming up."

Alarik waited until his brother slept to spring his trap. The moon was high before his brother breathed regularly beside him. Alarik stole naked into the yard and ran.

The trap gate had already fallen.

The vixen shrank back, snarling. When Alarik raised his hand the vixen erupted, leaping at the trap roof as if to tear that hand from its wrist, and Alarik paused again, half afraid that when he lifted the gate her dash would be, not for the safety of the woods, but for his throat. Her face was scarred and this increased its menace. A streak, where some rip had made the hairs grow back white, ran like a tear track from one eye to her upper lip; Alarik hadn't noticed that this afternoon.

Recollection of the cubs that awaited the vixen, of her expression as she had watched them, ended his irresolution.

The vixen scarcely seemed to touch earth as she fled. Alarik was so engrossed in the marvelous sight that he never heard his brother until he felt himself grabbed by the neck.

His father beat him. His mother gave him an empty dish for breakfast. "If you cared for eggs, you'd protect the hens!" His father and brother searched out the burrow on the sunny stream bank and brought five bodies home for Alarik to skin.

The vixen's face wasn't scarred at all.

The vixen he had freed from his brother's trap had not been the one he'd watched on the stream bank, the one his father had killed, but a witch.

The next time he'd seen her had been the week before his father's death. He'd seen her again the day before Lord Eurik's summons to war in Brittany.

Alarik let Storm and Luther bring him back to camp like a load of wood.

Some of the men had their dice out already. This camp

the king's daughter had ordained was suicidal—visible for
miles, within shooting distance of the woods—and the
men would all be drunk by sundown.

XII

December 584

VALRADA LAY ON HER BED, HER BREATH HEAVING WITH AN
occasional tired sniffle.

This was the first year since she's been old enough to
toddle after her mother with a branch or two in her arms
that she wouldn't help decorate the Hall for Christmas.
She had faced down the pain of her mother's absence and
gone out with the others to gather greens, but the smell
had made her sick and she had left without telling
Brunehaut more than that she was leaving. In her room
she wept tears of rage and frustrated hatred, eventually
subsiding to sniffles of self-pity—that the lovely smell of
fresh green boughs should now and ever after mean to
her not the blessed Lord's birthday, but the death of her
brother.

She'd told no one her suspicions about that death,
and this, perhaps as much as grief, was making her sick.

On her way out of the woods a dog fox had crossed her
path. Red-haired like Berto, it had looked at her steadily
for several moments before trotting off on silent paws.
She had stood staring after it, scarcely breathing. Hidden
in the heart of all Gaul's forests were camps of the swift-

footed race the Gallo-Romans had dispossessed before history began. These people, the Romans whispered, could turn themselves into foxes at will. When Valrada could move, she looked to see if the eerily silent creature had left tracks. They were plain in the snow. She had continued to the Hall reassured, but now that she'd exhausted herself crying, a sudden thought came like a blow on the back. Could Berto's soul, having died unshriven, be forced to inhabit the body of some witch's familiar? Were the masses they'd bought for his soul too few? Surely the priest knew the price of lifting a man of Berto's rank from purgatory to Heaven and wouldn't have understated it. But if Berto had been murdered. . . .

She'd said nothing direct in the confessional about her final meeting with Alarik or what had followed. She'd made the usual confession of disobedience and carnal thoughts, which the priest had heard as often as she had been able to arrange it since Alarik had offered to keep her deer. Unavenged murder was something the priest wouldn't be taking into account.

If Rikimer had planned Berto's death, could Berto be forced to run on four feet until Rikimer was punished? Now that Valrada reflected, she thought the dog fox's gaze had been reproachful. It had looked at her as if it knew her, as if. . . .

There was a knock at the door. Valrada sat up as the door opened. "Are you all right?" Brunehaut asked.

Valrada hunched over and began to rock. "My brother was murdered." Her jaws were stiff, but tears and words kept coming. "He was murdered, and I have done nothing."

Brunehaut closed the door.

It had been nearly four months since Valrada had sat in the great pine and watched Berto's borrowed spear part neatly over the wild boar's back.

Brunehaut listened, staring.

Valrada waited to be told not to jump to conclusions. She looked up in time to see Brunehaut's hand move mechanically to her womb. "Yes," said Valrada, "if it's a son you carry, he'll have to be protected from his dear cousin."

"Rikimer must be killed," Brunehaut answered.

Valrada's eyes were greener than absinthe, and bitterer. "Go ahead."

She had expected Brunehaut to dismiss her suspicions out of hand. She'd been framing the raging harangue with which she would greet this dismissal. She felt betrayed. If Brunehaut believed in Rikimer's guilt so quickly, she herself ought not to have spent all these months in doubt: She ought to have accused Rikimer before he escaped to Paris.

And just how was she to have accounted for her sylvan perch? She glared as Brunehaut opened her plump mouth again.

"Perhaps Alarik——"

"Yes, and perhaps my father," snapped Valrada.

When it came to challenging a treacherous fighter like Rikimer, Brunehaut needn't turn those wide blue eyes away from the fact that her own husband was father to the murdered man.

Valrada's words were the first reference to Lord Eurik that had passed between them since Brunehaut's hair had been braided. Brunehaut's eyes darkened implacably.

"Either you tell your father the day he comes home, or I will."

The room went gray. "Tell him what?" Valrada's voice cracked like an old woman's; she waited a moment to get it under control. "Tell him what I *think* I *might*, possibly, if my memory is right, have seen, sitting twenty feet up in a tree with my hair in my face and——"

"Tell him what you told me. Nothing's happened to your memory since I walked through that door."

"I want to see what Alarik thinks first. After all, telling my father won't bring Berto back to life."

"If your father comes back before Alarik comes back, then you must tell your father before you tell Alarik. Or I will."

"My father won't believe me! He'll think I just don't want to marry Rikimer and——"

"Well, you don't, do you? You must tell your father before one more word gets said about your marrying Rikimer!"

"You know how my father loved Berto; you know his temper as well as I do." Valrada rushed to cover that unfortunate choice of words: For a second she'd forgotten how much better Brunehaut had lately come to know Lord Eurik's temper. "If he attacks Rikimer we can't be at all certain Rikimer won't win."

Maybe that was what Brunehaut wanted. Maybe she was actually hoping Rikimer *would* kill Lord Eurik.

"Valrada, if Rikimer was a danger to Berto, then Rikimer is a danger to Berto's father. And not knowing it is an even greater danger to Berto's father."

Valrada scarcely heard Brunehaut's words for Brunehaut's voice, that Now-child-be-reasonable-like-me voice that Brunehaut took with her just about more often than Valrada could tolerate. Brunehaut was jealous of her, that was the problem, so miserable she was jealous of the pitiful amount of hope Valrada managed to keep alive that Alarik would come home from Toulouse in time and somehow make everything right before Rikimer and her father could come to terms. Valrada gripped her chair seat, trembling with rage. Jealousy was why Brunehaut was willing to make her betray her affair with Alarik.

Betray her affair. A terrifying realization washed through Valrada. Her skin went numb; her hands released their grip and hung. It wasn't her doubts of Rikimer's guilt that had been stilling her tongue, real as they were—not her fears that her father couldn't deal with Rikimer as Rikimer deserved, though these were equally real—but only her dread of confessing to her father that she had been meeting a young man. For this consideration, Berto's unavenged soul wandered.

"Tell your father," said Brunehaut, "that you were mushrooming."

The numbness in Valrada's skin crept inward; she sat frozen. She might have thought of this excuse herself. She had not—because at the thought of danger to Alarik, and, oh God, to herself, her mind had been paralyzed.

Meanwhile, her cousin was fighting side by side with her father. Brunehaut was right. She would be almost as guilty as Rikimer if her unwarned father died of Rikimer's treachery.

"I'll tell him," she whispered. "Now please leave me."

XIII

January 6, 584*

ON POIJOU'S HIGH ALTAR A CANDLE FLICKERED FOR THE VILLA'S absent lord, camped with his men outside the defiant walls of Tours. In Poijou's kitchen the Epiphany loaves were baked as always, each twelfth marked with a cross for the beggars who would knock at the door.

The first "beggar" was Alarik.

Alarik's Return, Valrada had pictured variously. In her favorite version, she had hurled herself in front of his snorting steed, which had stopped within a snowflake of her body, *which*, in turn, Alarik had leaped to the ground and clasped in his arms, in front of everyone. And this turned out to be all right because instead of coming straight home to Poijou, Alarik had detoured north and personally brought about the surrender of Tours, presenting its duke's head to the allied commanders on a pike. These commanders having rewarded him with half the duke's treasure, Alarik could now embrace just about anybody he chose.

Not every thought that idea conjured up was welcome, so at this point Valrada usually went back to the beginning and played that scene which she did like through again, with greater attention to detail.

In the real event, Alarik was in the Hall before Valrada knew it, and after the first gasp she found herself managing to greet him as formally as Brunehaut.

God should strike her barren that she was glad, only for a thoughtless second, that her mother wasn't there.

*It is still 584 because the Gallo-Roman year began in March.

She saw that her golden snake still twisted about Alarik's finger, and her heart leaped with a sharp, fierce pain. Her father's dogs crowded around Alarik, jumping, bumping, sniffing—just what the servants wanted to do: The hall teemed like a suet-hung tree. Valrada would have liked to raise her arms and send the whole flock flying. She turned despairing eyes on Brunehaut.

"We shall hear our guest's tidings beside my fire," Brunehaut pronounced. Valrada blessed her, not looking at Alarik. As she preceded him up the stairs, she took care to hold her head erect as a princess would, and to catch up the skirts of her plain gown with both hands as if its fringes were heavy with gold, not deigning, though for a horrid moment she was teetering, to reach out for the railing. She wondered if Alarik watched her, or only where he put his feet.

Those women who still fluttered about Brunehaut's room, Brunehaut sent for more wood, for wine, for almond cake. She herself stepped to the window and looked out at the tracks Alarik's horse had made in the courtyard. Alarik glanced once at Brunehaut's back and covered the distance to Valrada in two strides.

Brunehaut continued to consider those interesting tracks until the first slave's returning footsteps were heard in the hall—*and may the old witch be a slave forever,* was Valrada's silent prayer as Alarik hastily released her; *May she be lame in both legs for scurrying so!*

It was no old hag with the first tray, but Domnola the Breton. Valrada almost amen'd her curse aloud. The bright-eyed kitchen wench held her tray of bread and wine up to Alarik like something a little more than sacraments, and something considerably less. Valrada yearned to take the itch out of that tail herself, with a broom. She made an impatient noise and Domnola retreated to the wall where the other servants were gradually clustering.

Now Valrada was standing far enough from Alarik to look at him again herself. He'd gone home before presenting himself. There was no mud on his breeches and his beautiful blue mantle was not his warmest but his best. Valrada had reason to be grateful that he'd taken off his iron-ringed vest, but she rather wished he'd been unable to put off seeing her even long enough to knock the mud from his boots.

At least the delay surely meant that he had talked to someone, that someone had told him the worst that had happened at the Hall in his absence—the deaths; the wedding.

Had he realized, before Brunehaut met him with her hair in braids and Lady Chrona's keys hanging from her girdle, just who the bride had been? Brunehaut, Valrada noticed, had shrugged her braids behind her shoulders, where no doubt she hoped they were less conspicuous, and Alarik, now that Domnola had put food and drink in his hands, just stood looking at herself. The better to see her, or merely the better not to see Brunehaut? Valrada smoothed her skirts; she wished Brunehaut would say something before the servants began to speculate about this silence.

Sometimes when she had stolen to see Fleet in the pen behind Alarik's cottage he had sat on the grass beside her watching the young deer frolic for half an hour at a time without saying a word. That had been a companionable silence; this was choking. "We are hungry," Valrada managed to say, "for good news."

Alarik set down his cup and plate on the window ledge.

"Mine is bad." The fire snapped, and a log that had burnt through fell with two thuds on the hearth. "The entire south is in revolt. The Pretender has landed again."

Dread chilled Valrada. She knew that no one in Neustria should be surprised: A king's death always invited rebellion. They'd all half-known that Tours was only the beginning. Now in her mind's eye the ravens that flew black on gray across the sky became vultures, and the smoke from the chimneys of Poijou's huts became the smoke of the huts themselves.

Alarik began to pace. "We knew nothing of the assassination when we reached Toulouse. Evidently the Duke of Toulouse did know, but he'd told no one—no one but his fellow traitors!" Alarik's strides had brought him up against Brunehaut's clothes chest; he kicked it before he turned. "He persuaded the princess not to cross the border at once but to be his guest a few days, long enough to get her caravan freshened up. The Goths would laugh at her if her people had holes in their shoes, he said.

"He kindly placed her dowry in his vaults to keep it safe while her escorts got their stirrups polished.

"Those of us who turned back at Toulouse hadn't ridden half a day when we were overtaken by a gibbering messenger from its bishop. Our king was dead, and his daughter's dowry promised to his bastard brother to pay for this invasion." Valrada glanced uneasily at the servants. Had she been mistress, she would have sent them out.

"It's said the traitors are getting even more gold from Byzantium." Alarik slumped down on Brunehaut's clothes chest. "God knows how it will end."

There were steps and noisy talk in the hall. The woman

who burst panting into the room looked old until she lowered her hood to shake the snow from its folds, for though her hair was still black, her brown face was as wrinkled as the muzzle of a growling dog. The dogs of Poijou Hall did not growl at Antonia the midwife, whose smell they had known before they could see.

So had Valrada. She frowned, and frowned again as the door reopened and Claudia slipped into the room to melt in with the other servants. The dratted girl must have run straight to Antonia's hut the moment Alarik was sighted. For some reason, Claudia and the midwife had become great friends lately.

"Snowing," Antonia cried familiarly to Alarik. "Be glad your journey's ended." Then she leered.

Valrada flinched. In the years before Lord Eurik had brought the Greek doctor, Nicolaus, to Poijou, Antonia had delivered all Lady Chrona's children, Valrada included. Valrada hadn't felt able to refuse Antonia when she'd begged that Alarik be asked to inquire after her daughter, who had married a Bordeaux man. Valrada had realized at once that she'd promised too quickly. Why should Antonia turn to her for a good word with Alarik? It would have been wiser for Valrada to disclaim any influence with him, but she'd promised before she'd thought.

Old as Antonia was, she had come up the stairs so fast her cloak still sparkled with melted snowflakes. The sparkle in her eyes, Valrada couldn't avoid feeling, wasn't just from eagerness for news of her child.

"Your daughter is well," Alarik reported. "She has a fine son, a year come April."

Antonia cackled. "The wench, whelping in April like a she-wolf!" No one smiled, and one of the servants by the door whispered something in Antonia's ear. The old woman's head jerked backward like a parade leader's. "Traitors!" she exclaimed. "Swine!" She rounded theatrically on Alarik. "When do you ride against them? When do you drive this straggle-haired bastard back into the sea? Ah, if my young master lived, he would be armed, horsed, and——"

Alarik's face congealed. "If?" He turned to Valrada. "If?"

Valrada spread her hands, unable to make a sound.

After four months Valrada was no longer unable to utter Berto's name, but telling someone who hadn't heard put all the old weight on her tongue. Alarik, hemmed in by eyes and mouths, could not take her in his arms. She waved one hand in a helpless gesture at Brunehaut, and Brunehaut nodded. Her words to Alarik were obviously carefully calculated. "It was on a boar hunt."

Valrada began to cry, and Brunehaut sent the servants away.

He held her until she stopped shaking; "I didn't know. I didn't know."

"You hadn't been gone ten minutes," she said at last. "Not ten." She told him all that she seemed to have seen.

He listened, frowning, looking from Valrada to Brunehaut to the floor, at last slowly shaking his head. "There's just too little evidence against Rikimer. I think...you're looking for trouble. Berto is dead." She gasped that he could say it so easily, but he kept on talking, reasonable as always. "Berto's dead, and it's hard there's no one to punish. Of course you want to blame someone; that's normal. But you mustn't fool yourself. You know you've never liked Rikimer."

Her skin seemed to be tightening all over; she knew

now how a snake felt just before it slipped its glove. "Everybody else is so fond of him?"

"Because a man is unpopular doesn't make him a murderer. You have a habit of jumping to places you'd never be able to walk to, little one."

"But Rikimer *is* a murderer!" Valrada almost yelled, sending Brunehaut hurrying to check the other side of the door.

"I'll wait just outside," she told Alarik.

Valrada was beyond caring who heard her. "He killed my brother, and it was the death of my mother, and he might as well have killed Brunehaut and me the same day! You see yourself that Brunehaut can never be happy again, and my *father*," Valrada began to weep again, "my *father* wants *me* to *marry* Rikimer!"

Alarik stiffened and he seemed to grow taller and older in the space of a breath. "And what," he asked quietly, "does Rikimer say to that?"

That was better. Valrada threw herself into Brunehaut's chair. "Oh, he pretended he didn't want to force himself on me, but everybody knows he's just holding out for more dowry. My father and my uncle will have it all arranged between them before they march home. Nothing stopped them from coming to terms already except the war interrupted everything."

"The war, and your father's marriage."

Valrada stared. She had expected him to rant and roar, to throw her over his shoulder and climb out the window with her, not that the window approached being large enough, but *something* she had expected besides this cold reasoning.

"If Lady Brunehaut has a son, your father will forget about marrying you to your cousin."

She had counted on him. What was he, after all? *"And if she doesn't?"*

"We have months to think what to do then. Who knows what my share might be when we conquer Tours? I must get there at once."

"At once?" After four months? "But...my father is gone...and there's no one...there's no reason...Alarik! This may be our only chance in our whole lives to...to...just to be together like normal people instead——. Surely *one night?*"

"And risk having me miss a fight that might leave me rich enough to marry you? I must leave at once, Valrada."

"Then go!" she screamed. "Go now, this very second!"

Brunehaut stepped into the room and after that it was all quiet talk.

XIV

January 9, 584

THE DOVE PAIR WINTERING IN THE ORATORY RAFTERS BROKE OFF their purring monologues as Valrada entered. Valrada meant them no harm. Her mother had spared their nest in her last weeks, and Valrada hadn't let them be molested since. She lit the high altar's lamp, changed its spider-webbed cloth for a clean one, and knelt.

From the army, good news had been followed by bad before the good could be celebrated: Tours had surrendered, but Poitiers had followed it into rebellion.

Poijou's distance from the fighting had been halved. Prayer was called for, but Valrada could scarcely expect her prayers to be heard, so far was she from love and charity with mankind, so far from love and charity with *anyone*, anyone living. Her eyes drifted over the oratory's painted walls. Her mother, who could read a little, had sat most of one summer with the Life of Benedict of Monte Cassino unrolled in her lap, telling the painter how he should show that holy monk's miracles.

On one wall, Brother Benedict threw the wooden handle of another monk's pruning hook into a pond after its blade, which had flown off and sunk. In the next panel, the iron blade rose to the surface of the pond and rejoined its floating handle. People said that Benedict certainly had been a saint. Valrada certainly was no saint; she couldn't expect God to bless her throwing good after bad.

Would Berto understand this?

She could never face Berto in heaven. She had let him go unavenged all these months because she loved another man more than she loved him, her own brother. She knew she ought to be grateful to Brunehaut for making her see that, and sometimes she managed to be.

Just as she tried to be grateful to Alarik for being so very anxious to leave and fight for her.

Not even Brunehaut had been able to persuade him to promise to warn Lord Eurik against Rikimer. "Could anything make it more obvious that I love Valrada, than for me to come sidling up with a song and dance about my rival and not a shred of evidence, not even something I saw myself, but something she told me? 'How is it that my wife and my daughter confide in you?' Has either of you thought what I'm to say when he asks me that?"

He promised to be watchful himself; to watch over Lord Eurik; to watch Rikimer.

She must pray that this would be enough. She closed her eyes.

Something in the quality of the room changed. Her eyes flew open. The doves, she realized, had stopped gurgling. No one had come in, though that was the sort of feeling which had seized her—that she was suddenly not alone.

The light on the altar had gone out.

This, her heart tripped painfully, was a bad omen.

There were no drafts in the oratory to have blown out the lamp; the smoke from the incense always hung unstirred. A light going out of itself was a death omen. Whose? Valrada had a sudden vision of Rikimer, the skull in his topknot staring at her more insolently than Rikimer himself.

Briskly, Valrada rose. She must not have lit the lamp properly. She rekindled it.

The failing lamp hadn't been any sort of omen, it just needed its wick trimmed. The servants were taking advantage of a young mistress; the lamps were neglected. Valrada knelt again.

The dead lamp couldn't have been foretelling Alarik's death, he wasn't part of this household....

On the wall to her right, the abbot and his sister sat in the sister's garden talking of God, while rain and lightning raged outside their shelter.

The lamp on the Hall's high altar could only stand for the lord of this Hall....

The holy Benedict had refused his sister's plea to sit and talk with her all night, so she had prayed for Christ's help, and a storm had come from a cloudless sky and kept her brother at her side until dawn. Perhaps if Valrada's love for Berto had been great enough, heaven would have obliged her as it had Benedict's sister. Perhaps if she'd been anything approaching a saint, the iron of Berto's spear would have flown back to the wood as the pruning blade had done for Benedict.

Saintly she had never been, and certainly not to Berto.

She had constantly disobeyed Berto, tormented him with words—she'd always been quicker than he. In their nursery years she'd always manged to put the blame for things they'd done together on him alone. He was older and minded punishment less. She couldn't bear to be beaten, while he was neither so proud nor so afraid of pain. She had always given him her supper sweetmeats after such treachery, though he had never seen the connection because her escape from punishment and his suddenly major guilt had only baffled him, never made him suspicious of her. She really had been fond of him. He hadn't hit her since he was twelve. He had sat a horse better than any man on Poijou, except Alarik. Yes, she had loved Berto. The lamp on the altar burned steadily. Valrada shut her eyes. Through closed lids the flame was a red blur.

If she had once thought, that spring day, of what had been happening to her face since she'd begun that shameful secret bleeding, she would have ground the mushrooms into the earth with her heel. Instead she'd shown her harvest to Berto, expecting praise.

"They look like your face," he'd teased.

It had taken her a second, staring at the red-spotted caps, to realize what he meant. Her mother had vowed to her that no one noticed her lumps but herself.

She'd had no idea she would hit him. "Now you've got one yourself," she'd screamed, standing over him with her bloody crucifix still gripped as if she would knock him down again, should he rise, but he had laughed at her from the straw—as soon as he was sure she hadn't blinded him. Berto had cared nothing about scars, and anyhow his bangs had covered this one—until he lay dying. Valrada shuddered.

She began to pray to Christ and His spotless Mother to help her avenge her brother.

There was a whistling beat of wings over her head and Valrada looked up just in time to see one of the doves fly down from the rafters and extinguish the lamp on the high altar. She screamed a dry, almost noiseless scream and ran stumbling out of the oratory.

XV

January 14, 584

VALRADA'S EYES SMARTED FROM CROSS-HATCHING ONIONS, BUT AT last all were in the kettle, and she and Brunehaut waited, skimmers ready, for the butter to boil. Waiting made Valrada restless, but Brunehaut stood utterly still. Her sleeves were pinned up to protect them from being spattered, and her arms, folded across her apron, were pale as ivory. Her wide-open eyes, seemingly fixed on the melting butter, were as sightless as a carving's. She looked, Valrada decided, like some painted ivory saint, with the great carved skimmer as her symbol.

Valrada had said nothing of the dove and the lamp. Alarm, Antonia the midwife said, could bring Brunehaut's baby too soon. Whose failing light had the dove foretold? Five days had passed: Perhaps it had happened already. If Alarik or her father, it was her fault. Brunehaut's child? Brunehaut herself? Valrada's stomach felt the size of a fist.

The butter began to bubble.

The steward waited until the last onion was removed and the kettle lifted from the trivet to appear at Lady Brunehaut's elbow. "There's a child from the village, *mea Domina*. Samson the vinedresser's wife is ailing."

Valrada bent to wipe off her skimmer, to hide her relief. Seeing the steward enter the kitchen and come toward them so purposefully, she had thought at once and only of bad news from Poitiers.

Brunehaut sighed. "Say I'll come," she answered the steward, "when the butter is poured."

"Why not send me," Valrada offered. "It may be dark before this job is finished."

"Oh, would you go?

"Tell Claudia," Valrada instructed the steward, "to bring my cloak and boots." She would much rather get out of the Hall and walk than stay around the kitchen trying to match Brunehaut's serene facade.

Claudia could not be found.

No one had seen her since mass. The steward had thought she was with the weavers, the weavers had thought she was helping clarify the butter.

"I know where to look," Brunehaut said composedly. "Do not," she commanded her whispering women, "touch this kettle until I come back."

Brunehaut led Valrada unhurriedly to her own room,

and closed the door. "Have you any idea where she could be?"

"Antonia might. She and Claudia have been thick as thieves lately. I'll go to her hut after I've looked in on Samson's wife."

The morning before, Valrada had come upon Claudia vigorously scrubbing the stairs and exclaimed, "For goodness sake, you just scrubbed them yesterday. When my mother lived she could scarcely get you to clean them twice a month. You serve Lady Brunehaut better than you did my mother." Claudia had burst into tears. "She wouldn't run away over something like *that,* would she?" Valrada demanded. Her mother had unfailingly spoken kindly to all Poijou's servants; sometimes hearing how far short of that she herself fell, Valrada felt like hanging herself from a hook by her hair.

"Oh, she's been crying all winter."

"Yes, she has," Valrada said thoughtfully. Ever since her sister's "rape." Valrada had never mentioned that to Brunehaut.

"Is Claudia free, or a slave?"

"She was one of the three Mother freed last spring when Prince Clotar was born."

Brunehaut was relieved: Runaway slaves got their ears slit. "She still needs a paper to leave Poijou."

"She wouldn't need any Neustrian papers in Burgundy."

"How could she get all the way to the border without money?"

"Some one gave her a gold bracelet this summer."

Valrada left Samson's village hovel, cutting across the orchard toward Antonia's hut. Most women would have been afraid to live apart, on the edge of a woods, but

Antonia was so often called to deliver babies at night that she wanted to live, she said, where she could make up her sleep next day. "So Claudia's run off?" she cackled. "Well, at her age, it's with some young man."

"She spoke once of a younger sister," Valrada said, "but I don't remember the girl's name, and I never asked Claudia where she lived."

Antonia didn't know the sister's name either, she vowed, and couldn't remember where she was hired out.

The woods were dissolving in blue shadows and the orchard pruners were letting their bonfires die. The snow was crusting over. At a faint crackling in the woods behind her, Valrada looked back in time to see the white-tagged brush of a fox disappearing into the undergrowth. Valrada didn't believe in witches, because the priest had told her more than once that to do so was a sin. In any case, this fox plainly had its feet on the ground, for what she had heard had been its delicate little black paws breaking through the snow's ice sheen as it ran. Seeing the creature reminded Valrada, however, that she hadn't told Antonia that Samson's wife attributed her pain to some forest witch's spell.

The forest dwellers were a subject Valrada preferred not to have come up between her and the midwife. For some time she'd been almost half persuaded that some of Antonia's ointments came from the small dark women who knew what to say over herbs gathered by moonlight. This traffic, Valrada suspected, not a desire for quiet sleep, was why Antonia made her dwelling apart from the village.

There was no question, the forest folk were getting bolder. It was the monks' fault—or credit, if, like Alarik, you looked at it that way. For centuries the small people had kept themselves hidden and only the glowing in the sky at the year's four magic seasons had told the Romans with certainty that they were still there. Lately, since the time of Valrada's grandfathers, the Frankish monks had more and more often built their monasteries in wild tracts the Romans had never dared enter. These monks, who befriended the bear and the boar, had also sometimes befriended their wild human neighbors. "How else shall they ever be made Christians?" was Alarik's reaction, but Valrada had a feeling that to be made Christian, a folk must be possessed of souls.

Human or fey, forest folk were visiting remote villages even as much as annually now to barter. "Can we refuse salt to a fellow creature?" Alarik asked. *Should we provide iron to people who shoot from behind?* was what Valrada wondered.

She had heard it whispered (no one spoke ill of them out loud) that what a forest dweller couldn't make or buy he stole, whether tempered knife or hunting dog's puppy—or long-boned child. A village baby would outgrow his forest step-father—to throw a spear further, handle a longer bow. The forest girl who mated with such a youth would have larger children than her friends. It was said that when a Roman girl gave birth in secrecy and shame, she had only to leave the baby as deep in the forest as she dared to go, and it would be taken before the mother again saw open sky. It was said on the one hand that if she did not look back she would not be molested, and on the other that if she was well-born and well-possessed she might in time receive mysterious visits, undergo mysterious changes—always working yet never richer but always poorer, more grasping by the year, driven sometimes even to stealing. Of such a girl it was whispered that the forest dwellers had her soul. Yet many a girl thought it better to take that risk than to murder her infant, for which she would be irretrievably damned.

Valrada had grown cold; she hurried home to Poijou Hall.

XVI

February 584

THE MOST SHOCKING THING ABOUT THE GIRL IN ALARIK'S DREAM was that she had been Valrada. Ever since waking he'd kept as occupied as possible. All morning he'd worked like a foot soldier, hammering on the shelter they were building for their bore as if he were himself the bore, and battering already at the walls of Poitiers. Even then, like clouds scudding across the moon, his dream had darkened his mind as often as it had left him free. Now that he had to sit idle on this hillock he couldn't drive the images away. Beneath him Storm was restless, puzzled; all these men should either ride or dismount. Alarik stroked the black neck: He sympathized. In fact, he half wished Storm would rear, buck, do anything to drive the naked girl out of his mind.

"The pigs want driving," Rikimer said. It was true that so far the state of the infantry below much more resembled slop time than a disciplined army forming to attack. At Rikimer's voice his stallion leaped forward and Alarik set his jaw as Rikimer jerked the confused animal back.

Alarik would never have gelded Storm. He laid his hand on the gelding's neck again, like a mother putting her arm around a homely daughter when a pretty child walks by.

Alarik had acquired Storm on the battlefield of Vannes, to some newly widowed Breton's loss. Badly gashed, the black horse would have been destroyed had Alarik not claimed it. Through good fortune it had been standing, half dazed, near Alarik's own mount where it lay, stiff on its back like an overturned foot stool. A Breton had gutted Alarik's mount on the first charge, hurling himself on Alarik's very spear point to get at the poor beast. What was left of light that evening Alarik had spent stitching up the black gelding.

The trees on the hillock were slender and bare; Alarik wished the wind that blew through them would blow the girl's face away. Down below, the infantry banners flapped.

"I dreamed last night we burned through their gates today," Lord Eurik's brother, Lord Dag, volunteered.

Alarik, wincing at his own dream, missed Lord Eurik's reply.

"They say dreams have meaning," Lord Dag insisted. "Do you never dream?"

"Never," said Eurik.

The hollow boom of war horns echoed up to them and more men scrambled into place down below. Alarik tested the thong on his lance. Soon. Lord Dag dismounted and walked over to a tree—the third time. Alarik had the same feeling, but in this company he would sooner wet his breeches.

Alarik's great-grandfather had won his freehold at Poitiers, not eighty years ago. Alarik might win a Lord's daughter today. It was only a question of wealth, and Poitiers was a golden city.

Eighty years ago the enemy had been Visigoths: heretics, aliens, as in Brittany. Today would be like Tours. Nothing had distinguished Tourian from friend but the cry: "Clotar!" or "Childebert!" and the sword did or did not swing. Alarik closed his eyes.

He opened them again at once as the girl he had stripped in his dream struggled again before them. "Lord God," he exclaimed. "The Burgundians are using oxen!"

Waves of cheering broke from Burgundy's ranks as their bore slowly drew ahead of them and began its ponderous advance on the walls—not propelled by the men beneath its shelter, but drawn by unsheltered oxen. Beside Alarik, Lord Eurik was grinning. Alarik's hands twisted in Storm's mane. "They'll be cut to fish bait!"

"Yes," said Lord Eurik.

Alarik felt the sweat prickle on his forehead. He put on his helmet—to be moving, to hide some of his face. The men around him leaned forward in their saddles to watch their allies trudge to disaster.

There was not a sound from Poitiers.

To the horsemen on the hillock, the hide-covered penthouse sheltering the Burgundians who were to work the bore had the appearance of a sow's back. From beneath it the great iron-pointed pole protruded like a tusk. Alarik looked at Rikimer, whom Valrada had accused of working with the tusk of a boar. Was it only because Valrada had been offered to Rikimer that Rikimer looked so ugly to him?

Rikimer's bony face was as grim as the skull on his topknot pin, his eyebrows so white that even at Alarik's distance they were barely visible. His mustache, more conspicuous because it was fuller, wasn't full enough to conceal his mouth—the mouth of a young man who has perceived since tiny childhood that his father loves his brothers and even his sisters better than himself, and his mother loves Jesus better than any of them. Had he contrived his cousin's death? Alarik wished there were more horsemen than Lord Dag between Lord Eurik and his nephew.

He wished he weren't going to have to confess to the priest that he had most heartily wished a fellow oathman death in battle.

The bore rolled ever closer to the city walls, followed at a smug distance by the foot soldiers, who planned to rush in through the hole they expected it to make. The rebels were absolutely quiet as the big oxen plodded nearer. Alarik's mouth was dry.

Suddenly every archer on the northern wall let fly. Like swallows, a dark cloud of arrows rose and swooped. In a moment, every ox floundered in the snow.

"The Burgundian sow has farrowed," said Lord Eurik. From under the stalled shelter, men were scampering, and more arrows cut some of them down. They writhed in the snow like wallowing piglets.

Alarik's hand tightened on his spear and his lips began to move. *Angels that run between the stars, give strength to my horse in this battle, that he shall not be tired and he shall not stumble and no weapon shall touch him and——*. A roar from the walls and the gates of Poitiers swung open. Rebel cavalry poured out onto the broad causeway, shrieking to God and St. Hilary, and charged the stunned Burgundian foot. Alarik's lips stopped moving.

Snow from Storm's hoofs splattered Alarik to the waist; the wind whistled past. A neck behind, Lord Eurik was yelling like a madman. He saw Alarik look back and waved his shield. Lord Dag was still between him and Rikimer. The horses swept on with a noise like the surf, flanking the Burgundians. The rebels wheeled and charged to meet them. An arrow whined past Alarik's shoulder. He ducked his head down further behind his shield and chose his man. The rebel carried his shield low, but Alarik never liked aiming for a face. The head could dodge too easily. Alarik's spear point took the rebel on the shoulder and lifted him out of his saddle.

Storm bucked and Alarik freed his spear. He wanted to finish the rebel but a bay was bearing down on him. Storm faced the bay. Its rider's teeth were bared, his helmet crest stiff like the ruff of a snarling dog. Then his shield hid him. Alarik flung his spear underhand and took the bay in the chest. The poor beast crashed on its head: The rider was thrown under Lord Dag's hoofs. Alarik drew his sword and in the moment he had to breathe, looked back for Lord Eurik. He saw the arrow hit Lord Eurik in the face.

Jesus, Mary——. Storm reared and Alarik turned just in time to parry an ax blow with his sword. He brought the sword down, and arm and ax fell together. Blood painted Storm's side. Alarik's pulse was drumming in his ears and lights flared and plunged before his eyes. He tried to turn Storm, to get back to Lord Eurik before the tribune was trampled. He choked on admitting Lord Eurik was already dead. Panting, almost convulsively, he looked back.

Lord Eurik was upright in the saddle. The arrow shaft projected from between his eyes: It shook as he rode. He laid about with his sword.

A moment, and Alarik no longer knew if he'd seen this sight or not. Storm, trained to meet attack, would not wheel. Another rebel was charging Alarik. Their swords rang together and in the instant before their horses collided, Alarik's blade spun away. The collision knocked both horses to the ground. Alarik struggled to get free and rise. He had made it to one knee when the other man regained his feet and came at him. Alarik flung his javelin and sprang upright. He had only his dagger left. The rebel caught the barbed javelin on his shield: Alarik leaped to get his foot on the javelin butt, forcing the rebel's shield downward. He parried the rebel's sword swing and gave his neck a deep gash. He jumped aside as the man fell.

Someone was trumpeting. Where was Lord Eurik? The rebel horsemen were retreating. Alarik's comrades swept around and past him, chasing them. Storm floundered to his feet and ran away with the rest.

Alarik's skull pounded. He shook his head to clear his sight. The ravens that had circled joyfully above the battle were already settling.

Was Lord Eurik among those who had thundered past? As for Rikimer, Alarik hadn't seen him since the charge.

Alarik staggered over to the horse Storm had felled. Ravens had found it. Its head kept straining to bite at the ravens and then falling back in the snow. The horse was done for. Its great eyes were pitiful. Alarik found his sword and killed the horse quickly.

He heard shouts at a distance and realized that the Burgundian foot were coming, to strip the dead the

Neustrians had killed. And those the rebels had killed.... Alarik went to the rebel whose shield still held his javelin: He retrieved that, and he took the rebel's mailed vest. If Storm didn't get back, he would buy a horse with it.

And if Lord Eurik didn't get back?

The snow was red a wide way around the rebel's head. Alarik realized that his knees were trembling and he cursed the Burgundians running toward him.

XVII

Same day

THE SURGEON CAME OUT OF LORD EURIK'S TENT. HE HURRIED away without looking at Alarik or Lord Eurik's tent boys, who stood in the snow. Lord Dag came to the opening. He motioned Alarik in.

Lord Eurik was sitting on his cot. As he turned his head to see who was coming, the arrow shaft swayed up and down in front of his face. Above it in the center of his forehead his birthmark was like a burn. "Give me another drink," he demanded.

Alarik thought Lord Dag was going to cry. "The surgeon won't touch him," Lord Dag said.

Alarik walked over to Lord Eurik. The arrow had entered between the nose and right eye. It would be barbed: They would never draw it out. It wouldn't come; or if it came, it would bring everything with it.

Neither could it be cut out. No surgeon would dissect a man between his eye and his nose.

Lord Eurik glared back at Alarik. "Better a dead lion than a living dog," he growled, and looked away.

Alarik felt the back of Lord Eurik's neck. He pressed with his fingers where he thought right. He felt nothing, however, and Lord Eurik made no sound. "Do you feel pain!"

"Christ's warts, of course I feel pain!"

Alarik glanced at Lord Dag, but Lord Dag's anguished eyes were glued on the bobbing arrow. "I mean here," Alarik said, pressing again.

"There," gritted Lord Eurik.

Alarik stood back. "You'll live," he said, "and keep your eye." Lord Eurik blinked at him. "Get him drunk," Alarik told Lord Dag superfluously.

The wine rippled wildly in the cup: Lord Dag's hands were trembling.

Lord Eurik's were steady.

Alarik took off his cloak, folded it, and laid it on top of Lord Eurik's saddle. He inspected his sheath knife: It would cut an eyelash. He wouldn't blunt its edge on wood. "Give me yours," he told Lord Dag. "Hold still," he told Lord Eurik, "my lord." He set Lord Dag's little blade against the invading shaft as close to Lord Eurik's nose as possible. As he cut, he was acutely conscious of the golden snakes that tried to meet around his smallest finger. Valrada's eyes as she had given him the ring had been wide as the ocean. Lord Eurik's were closed.

Abruptly the knife won through and Alarik dropped the suddenly small-seeming fledged stick on the floor.

Lord Eurik bent and picked it up. He examined it expressionlessly, riffling his thumb against the feathers.

"Drink, my lord." Alarik returned Lord Dag's knife. He stepped to the tent flap and told the miserable tent boys to get hot water. The boys exploded into arms and legs. He wished he could send the boys to look for Storm. Lord Eurik had his head in his hands; he was about ready.One of the boys came in with hot water and the second with a basin; either could have carried both. The boys stood close together, gaping at Lord Eurik. Alarik washed his hands. Suddenly as he dried them the girl's face was clear again, under them, and other things, under them, but it was the dream's face that burned him worst because the—other things could have been anybody's. If he should be punished for his dream with failure now....

"She's pregnant!" Lord Eurik lifted his head. Lord Dag stuck the cup in front of him and he swallowed twice before his head flopped back into his hands. "She might have claimed it to be rid of me," Lord Eurik muttered through his fingers, "but it's true, she is. Wine," he added, and his brother leaned over to give it to him. He sucked. "Offered him slaves, cattle, vineyards. Sat there sucking his damned teeth. Know what he wants, wants jewels. Warned him. Warned him, best offer. Warned him what I'd do. Thought I was too old." One elbow slid off Lord Eurik's knee and he couldn't seem to replace it. Lord Dag eased him face-down onto his cot. The boys inched closer. Alarik took the bucket from the first and set it beside the cot. He took the basin from the second and gave it to Lord Dag. "Out," he told the boys. When they were gone, hating him, he put his right knee on Lord Eurik's cot and his left hand on Lord Eurik's left shoulder and drew his own sheath knife again.

In the dream he had both done and seen himself doing. Now he saw only the point of his knife. He cut open the skin at the back of the head where Lord Eurik had felt the most pain. The arrowhead was very close to the skin. He drew it out, point first.

Lord Dag's tent boy Lupus was waiting with Lord Eurik's boys. He had Storm by the bridle.

Lord Eurik's boys thrust themselves in front of Alarik, staring up into his face like hungry dogs. Alarik looked over their heads at his horse. "Burn these," he told the boys.

Alarik wanted to hug Lupus. He gave him two coppers.

"Odo Lehunsson knew him for yours and brought him," Lupus said.

There was nothing wrong with Storm that tar wouldn't fix. Alarik wanted to see to it himself, but over the horse's withers he saw coming that damned deacon of Rikimer's. "Tar those places," Alarik handed Storm's bridle back to Lupus, and stepped between the deacon and Lord Eurik's tent.

"My lord Rikimer sent me," the deacon purred, "in case his uncle needed a priest."

"It's over," said Alarik.

The deacon crossed himself. His face took on the gravest of his minstrel's range of expressions, but before he could avow his sorrow a roar from inside the tent dropped his fat lower lip.

"Wine!" came Lord Eurik's unmistakable voice. Alarik observed the deacon's disconcertion but was too angry to be amused.

"The surgeon has triumphed?" the deacon asked with incredulous joy. "Lord Eurik will fight again?"

"Lord Eurik will do everything he's ever done," Alarik said pointedly.

Lord Eurik's boys were returning on the run: Alarik sent them into the tent with a jerked thumb. He stepped toward the deacon to let the boys enter behind him, making the deacon fall back. "By chance the arrow missed his brain. It came out readily."

"By chance—as some call the Grace of God."

Alarik dutifully crossed himself, inwardly damning the deacon straight to hell. "The eye was untouched," he piled it on. "Lord Eurik's face won't even be scarred."

"Our old friend the animal doctor," the deacon said sourly. "Your uncle will ride again within the week; he didn't even lose much blood."

"'By chance the arrow missed his brain,'" Rikimer mimicked. "His brain wasn't big enough for the arrow to find. You see the same problem at pig-sticking, every winter."

The deacon made a face.

XVIII

Early March 585

THE WHOLE CAMP WAS A MUDBOG, BUT UNDER THE HORSE LINE was worst. The restless animals had churned their footing to black dough.

"Mine's standing wrong," Eurik said.

Dag left Lupus to feed his roan and went down the line to where Eurik and his tent boys stood scowling at Eurik's stallion.

The stallion had the weight off one foreleg. Eurik swore under his breath and stepped into the kneaded mud. He ran his hand down each leg, the lifted leg last. "Heat?"

Eurik didn't answer. He pulled the favored leg forward and backward as far as it would go, and before he could do it again the stallion was snorting on its hind legs.

"Probably just a stone bruise," suggested Dag. That was the least serious lameness a horse could have, and Eurik's luck was always good. Look at him: Three weeks ago he had stared into his grave, an arrow sticking out of him like a moon colt's horn. Eurik was bent over the questionable forefoot. Dag contemplated the back of his neck, which hadn't even stayed bandaged long enough for the skin to pale. The breeze from the river cut Dag's left thigh like the knife that had taken the Breton arrow out, five *years* ago. Dag rubbed the scar through his breeches.

"Aagh." Eurik let go the foot; it was coated well above the fetlock with sticky mud. "Can't tell a damned thing. Damned sty." He wiped his hands on his breeches. "Water and rags," he dispatched one of his boys, "to the orchard." Eurik jerked his head in the direction of a field of apple trees just north of camp. He slipped the knot from the line and handed his stallion's rope to the other boy.

Dag skwushed off after Eurik. Dag's head ached. He'd had a strange dream. He tried to remember that he'd been just as worried at Tours, but he'd never before dreamed a thing like this. Why had the One-eyed god appeared to him, when it was Eurik their father had dedicated? Such a dream was supposed to mean victory or death, and it was supposed to be all the same to the dreamer which one, if the One-eyed god, the Spear-lord and Host-father himself, gave it. Dag, however, wondered which.

Eurik hadn't been worried at Tours. "We took Tours seven years ago," was all he'd had to say. How much did his assurance owe to that dedication thirty years ago when their father had returned from the Saxon rebellion, looked at his two sons, and chosen Eurik? Ever since, all the Host-father's help had gone to Eurik, he was always lucky in battle, and battle luck gave a man other luck.

The footing was relatively firm in the orchard because no one went there: From miles around, the serfs had all taken refuge in Poitiers.

"Trot him," Eurik told his boy.

The boy began to run with the horse, back and forth in front of Eurik. Eurik folded his arms and watched. Every time the right forefoot touched ground the stallion raised its head.

"It hurts him, all right," Dag said.

Eurik grunted.

The second boy came with a bucket.

"Tie him there," Eurik told the first boy. One minute later he set the cleaned foot down. "Stone bruise," he said.

XIX

Late March 585

OH, MARY, BRIGHT AND BEAUTIFUL, AVENGE ME ON MY COUSIN! Valrada knelt alone before the oratory's high altar. At a rustling overhead her eyes flew open. She would have those doves torn out before Vespers! What was to become of Brunehaut and herself? If *they* were to be turned out, why should the doves remain?

God, that a man's skull could be crushed as quickly as an egg!

Valrada shifted her knees with a shuddering sigh. If she'd been a judicious person like Brunehaut, Alarik would have believed what she said about Rikimer, would have protected her father. Guilt put another twist in her grief-knotted stomach. She ought to have told her father himself, ought to have told him six months ago. Might God forgive her, might the rebels *gut* Rikimer! *Lord God of mercies, forgive my father's sins and receive him in peace.*

Eurik's body wouldn't be brought home for burial, Rikimer had told Valrada and Brunehaut. There was no time. "The Pretender is camped on the banks of the Dordogne with a large army, and we march in haste to engage him. I rode ahead, because I couldn't bear to think of your hearing of our common tragedy but from someone who mourns him as keenly as yourselves."

Valrada let go of her prayer beads and wiped her face.

"We buried my uncle at Poitiers," Rikimer had told her and Brunehaut, "which he helped us conquer."

Rikimer claimed that her father had been killed by rocks hurled from the walls of Poitiers, but Valrada wouldn't believe this until she heard it from Alarik. Why had Alarik let her hear this first from Rikimer?

If it came to that, why had she gone off and left Brunehaut alone to put up with Rikimer's odious feigned sympathy?

Because she had felt that two more minutes in his presence would have her shrieking. There was no use pretending Brunehaut minded this death as she did. For Brunehaut it was in some part a deliverance.

One look at Brunehaut confirmed Rikimer's fears: There was a maggot inside this peach. If it turned out to be a son, he, not Rikimer, would be heir to Poijou. He should have taken his father's advice, for once, and married Valrada.

But who could say his aunt wouldn't have died anyway?

Brunehaut, Brunehaut was surprised to hear, had been the object of Rikimer's ardent desire for a long time. Rikimer had almost summoned his courage to speak to her, he confessed, when suddenly Lord Eurik had asked him to marry Valrada. "I knew that if I said how I worshipped you and could marry no other, his anger would fall on you." Then, when Lord Eurik had married Brunehaut himself, Rikimer had despaired. "It is mortal sin to covet another man's wife. I welcomed the fighting that took me far from Poijou. I knew that every glimpse of your ineffable face would imperil my soul."

Brunehaut turned her ineffable face toward Domnola, who sat beside the door, to remind Rikimer that the girl was there.

Brunehaut's beauty was such, Rikimer insisted, she could only be a creature of Paradise.

Under Brunehaut's folded hands her child rippled from time to time. She knew her tunic wasn't so loose that Rikimer didn't see how small her lap had shrunk. This would have been beautiful to Lord Eurik, but she wouldn't have predicted that any other man would view her swelling quite that way. "What you ask is out of the question," she interrupted Rikimer. "By my marriage to Lord Eurik, I am your aunt."

Rikimer had hoped the cow wouldn't think of that. He was in a hurry; the Neustrian army would pass Poijou in two days. "We can get a dispensation. The Duke wants my father and me to fight the Pretender; he'll have the bishop himself perform our marriage, if you wish."

"The bishop may put the host to my lips, but if I've committed mortal sin, it's only saltless bread to me. No bishop can pray a soul out of hell; only Christ can do that, and why should Christ pardon a soul as unworthy as mine?"

"Ah, lady," Rikimer sighed at last, "if you knew how desperate the thought makes me that I may never take you in my arms, you would fear to turn me away, lest in my despair I do some rash thing that will damn me." Rikimer, who meant to be hinting at suicide, was unaware of the sinister impression his words made.

"I should very likely be struck dead at the altar, and then what of my unborn child? Dying, I should be my own baby's murderess."

It was an attractive picture, but Rikimer had no chance to speak. There was a knock and Domnola reluctantly opened the door to the steward, who had time to say "My lady, there is——" before he was lifted bodily by the shoulders and set to one side by the man behind him.

Alarik hadn't even stopped downstairs to hand a servant his cloak. "In the oratory," Brunehaut told him. Alarik saluted Rikimer and strode back down the hall.

Rikimer gazed thoughtfully after him.

Tears overwhelmed Valrada the moment she was in his arms. "You're all I have, now." How had Brunehaut stood the last four years? For Brunehaut there had been no comforting cloak to hide her from the world, no shoulder.

They did nothing in the oratory they hadn't done in St. Eustace's chapel, and God hadn't blinded them there. At last, Valrada began to ask the inevitable questions.

Alarik held her tightly, so as not to see the pain his words gave. "I saw the rock strike him. His stallion was crazy that day; it would have fought on ice. I was only a little behind him when suddenly the beast charged and I was left, and then it was over. Your father hadn't given his yell, so I think perhaps the stallion had the bit between its teeth, but who can be sure...your father was dauntless when he was angry."

Was. Valrada pulled free of Alarik's arms and sank onto one of the benches. "What will my uncle do now? Will he make me marry Rikimer?"

"Valrada, I believe your uncle is fonder of you than he is of Rikimer."

"Fond! Who is he frightened of, that's the question! No one is afraid of me, and everyone is afraid of Rikimer!"

She saw his ears lift as the skin of his forehead pulled back; she hadn't meant that "everyone" to needle him. "Until the prince's regents," he said tightly, "confirm the passing of your father's land to your uncle, Lord Dag can do nothing. The dukes won't act till Brunehaut's child is born, because if she bears a son, your uncle will be guardian only."

Valrada knew all that. "It's all the same so far as you and I are concerned—unless you want to wait twelve years to marry me!" In twelve years, if Dag refused them meanwhile, they might humbly ask Brunehaut's son.

"I wouldn't wait twelve weeks if it weren't for this rebellion, but I have to rejoin the army in four days at most."

"Oh, I curse this Pretender in my dreams! Why did King Clotar stop at his hair when he disowned him, why didn't he cut off his head?"

Alarik shrugged.

"What will Rikimer do while we wait for Brunehaut's baby? Do you think he'll have my uncle turn us out?" Dag, if he wished, could put any of his oathmen in Poijou Hall. Valrada and Brunehaut would have to move to Antier. "I can *not live* under the same roof with Rikimer!"

"Until the regents act, Lord Dag can do nothing."

Valrada sighed. "Do you think my uncle will let us marry?"

"We'll marry. I shall make his consent a condition of my fealty."

"And if he refuses?"

"I commend myself to a stronger lord, and come and *get* you." He pulled her up to him again.

Rikimer rode without looking back. The muscle in his left cheek twitched spasmodically. His uncle was laughing in hell.

Refused, *refused* him, with her self-righteous mooing about the church! He'd never known she could put so many words together without stopping to chew her cud. Christ this and the bishop that. She seemed to forget the child could be a girl.

Whoever wound up with Poijou after Brunehaut whelped was going to have to pay some parasite to take Valrada off his hands; whether the parasite was a convent or that ox in the oratory with her this minute, wouldn't alter the price. If Brunehaut had accepted him, *he* would have had to pay it, and he could imagine the sum, with both women and his father ganging up on him. His father had a weakness for pretty women, Valrada included. But if Rikimer married Valrada himself, the dowry was his.

He had done the generous thing by Brunehaut. He had offered to give his little cousin a father—but he wouldn't offer again. He was well out of it. Valrada was the bride for him. Prettier, and never any nonsense out of her about Jesus. A hellion, but he could beat that out of her.

June 585

DOMNOLA'S CURLS FELL FORWARD OVER HER FACE AS SHE WORRIED the sheets in the river. The curls hid a scowl, Valrada was sure. All the household women were annoyed with Brunehaut for making them launder directly after a week's rain. Lady Chrona had always given the river mud a day to settle.

As always at the thought of her mother, Valrada's insides tightened. Her mind, despite her, veered to the spear that in killing Berto had caused her mother's death, too; she shut her eyes and took five deep breaths, concentrating on not asking herself what to do about it. That question was what was making her thin as a spear herself, as if every time she answered "I don't know" it cut a little piece off her.

She opened her eyes and concentrated, hard, on what she saw.

Brunehaut sat knitting with her back against a willow tree, her pet kid dozing beside her. Smooth faced, she looked as oblivious of her women's sullen mood as he.

The more pregnant Brunehaut got, the more oblivious

to everything she seemed, Valrada thought. Domnola's wooden beads, for instance, were obviously hanging in the way of her work, and it was Brunehaut's place to make her take them off.

Domnola, however, had hung the little iron cross Lady Chrona had given her on the same string as her painted beads. If she removed her string of beads, she would also be removing her cross, which Brunehaut would be the last to suggest.

Domnola's claim of Christianity was as transparent as the amber she had worn the day Lady Chrona bought her, Valrada suspected. Wearing amber was against the church law.

Lady Chrona had happened to pass through the marketplace during the auction of some Breton captives. One had thrown herself on her knees and caught Lady Chrona's skirts. "Buy me, buy me, I'm a Christian," she'd cried before the auctioneer could jerk her to her feet. Lady Chrona had tried to question the girl, but Domnola's plea, it seemed, was the only Frankish she'd known.

"Probably the only Christianity she knows, too," Lord Eurik had jeered when Lady Chrona brought her home.

Since the new slave was pretty, Eurik hadn't grumbled much. Her name was something unpronounceable, so Lady Chrona called her Domnola.

Lazy thing should have been named *Somnola*, Valrada thought. Anybody looking at her would think she was soaking her wrists, not laundering.

Brunehaut paid no attention. She was so absorbed in her interminable knitting that she didn't even notice Basil wake up and start nibbling the ends of her braids.

Valrada had named the kid B-a-a-sil because that was

what his mother called him. Then his mother had died and the name wasn't amusing anymore. Tears welled in Valrada's eyes. That was one death her tenderhearted mother hadn't lived to see.

Valrada stood up and gave her skirts a shake. She was getting like Claudia, before Claudia took herself off, crying all the time.

Basil deserted the unresponsive Brunehaut and skipped daintily to Valrada's side, braced his legs, and began to rub his head against her knee. She scratched the two itching horn-bumps for him, and he leaned gratefully into the motion, pressed, finally, against her leg, a comforting warmth.

"Someone's coming!" Domnola called from the riverside. Brunehaut's head jerked around.

"It's only Mummolus, one of our huntsmen," Valrada quickly assured her. One would have thought Brunehaut expected Rikimer, with a dragon for a mount and the devil himself for a deacon. "Mummolus was Berto's favorite."

The hunstman strode purposefully toward them.

"He's bringing something," Brunehaut said.

The huntsman didn't even glance at Poijou's mistress, but presented his kill, a woodcock, to Valrada. Valrada opened her mouth to correct him. Something harder than feathered flesh pressed her fingers and when she parted them to see what, she closed them again instantly and her mouth as well.

She had almost dropped a two-headed golden snake ring.

Her vision blurred, dazzled by a sun that suddenly filled the sky. "Where," she forced her voice not to tremble, "did you find it?"

"The dogs flushed it," the huntsman answered levelly, "near that old chapel to St. Eustace."

Valrada needed something to lean on. Her ears hummed. "I'll take the bird to the kitchen right away," she told Brunehaut.

"Let him——" Brunehaut started. "Good," she finished.

Valrada was careful to keep hold of the dead bird while she and Mummolus were within Brunehaut's sight. Keeping up the show of conversation which Brunehaut had obviously guessed she wanted to have with Berto's friend, was unexpectedly hard. "Is the war over? Did we win?"

"We spoke of nothing but my errand to you, *mea Domina*. He said that time was everything."

"Was he well? How did he look?

Mummolus shrugged.

Valrada wanted to shake the man.

"I did see his horse, *mea Domina*. It looked hard ridden."

Once beyond the field's high hedge, Valrada gave Mummolus back his woodcock to take to the steward and turned her almost dizzy steps toward the chapel in the forest.

If the fighting were over, Alarik could return openly. So it was not. Worse, it must be getting close to Poijou for Alarik to think he could come and go back before he was missed. Fear made the breath harsh in Valrada's throat. He was coming to warn them to flee. *How*, with Brunehaut eight months pregnant?

He was sweat-stained and dirty and the most beautiful thing Valrada had seen since spring. When he lifted her in his arms, she felt all her woes drop from her like a leaden cloak falling.

But he put her down.

She began to remember some of her questions.

At his first answer, the chapel floor seemed to tilt under her feet.

"The war is over; the Pretender is dead."

She gaped at him, speechless.

"His own men killed him. King Gontram had promised them pardons in exchange."

"Pardons!" In *March* Alarik had left her for what might have been forever, all because of the southern dukes' treachery. Two months—more than two months—she had lost of him, months she could never get back. "The king should promise every traitor his head and then give it to him on a plate!"

"Our army and Gontram's are marching to Paris to see Prince Clotar acknowledged our throne's heir. They take the Limoges road and won't pass by Poijou; I left at dusk last night just—to see you. But if I'm missed, if I'm caught, I'm a deserter. So for today, it's hello and farewell. I must catch them before they reach Paris."

"But you have—have a few hours, surely? An *hour?*" Her voice rose as his face said no for him. "How can you just kiss me and be off? Don't you have any feelings for me at all, don't you have any feelings whatever? Alarik, one of us two must be a monster!"

His jaw remained rigid; she stroked it with her fingertips. "Listen," she whispered. "No one knows we're here. Who is there for miles who could do anything, who would even say anything, if he guessed? But no one even will know, no one ever will guess. Just this once, just this once." She leaned forward, brushing against him. "We're going to marry anyway, aren't we? Aren't we?"

He took both her hands prisoner. "It's a sin.

"It's a crime.

"What if you get pregnant? I don't know how long we'll be kept in Paris. First, the bishops must gather from every corner of Gaul. Then, when they've blessed the queen's boy, he'll be christened with all the pomp she can buy. There'll be weeks of feasting.

"All that done at last, Gontram will march his army back to Burgundy, and we Neustrians can disband ours and come home—Gontram says. What if his resolve falters? What if we have to strengthen it for him? What will become of you if I'm killed and you're pregnant?" His grip on her hands tightened. "Pray for us. I should be home before autumn."

"And then...?"

"And then."

As Valrada emerged from the forest, a vixen with a dead gosling in its mouth trotted across her path. One of Antonia's goslings, Valrada realized, but she forgave the murderess. Alarik said that a vixen's forays were boldest when she had cubs to feed.

The sheets were spread to bleach on the riverbanks. Basil came running to meet her. Brunehaut, she saw with relief, was gone.

"My lady," Domnola told her at once, "your cousin, Lord Rikimer, was here."

It hadn't occurred to Valrada that what Alarik could do, Rikimer could do.

"The steward couldn't say where you might be, and Lady Brunehaut was taking her nap...."

"So you woke Lady Brunehaut?" Valrada smacked Basil's nose to make him stop rubbing his infernal head against her knee. The risk Alarik had taken only with extremest caution, Rikimer had taken openly.

"No, my lady, Lord Rikimer said on no account should she be distrubed. He only wanted to know all was well with us."

Real foxes didn't hunt by day, cubs or no.

The vixen had had a vertical white streak down one cheek, from just below her eye to the corner of her mouth—a scar, probably, where the hair had grown in white. Valrada shuddered, remembering, now, what bad luck it was to injure a fox and not kill it. Left alive, a witch always avenged injury.

There had been contempt in the vixen's yellow eyes as it trotted off deeper into the forest with Antonia's fledgling in its jaws—contempt, as if it knew Valrada for one too weak to take vengeance.

Valrada's heart stopped dancing. "How long was Lord Rikimer here?"

"Oh, not long, my lady; he had to get back to the army before he was missed. The army——"

"Did the steward welcome him properly?" If Domnola wondered why Valrada wasn't slathering for news of the army, let her wonder.

"Oh, yes, my lady. Greek Nicolaus drank the farewell cup with him, quite properly. Lord Rikimer bade me say how sorry he was to miss you, my lady."

Valrada's eyes narrowed. Did she imagine that the Breton looked sly?

"Lord Rikimer sent me to Antonia's to see if you were there, but when you weren't he couldn't wait any longer."

There were two gold beads in Domnola's necklace, one

on each side of the iron cross. They were new, new since morning.

She should be sold.

Brunehaut insisted it was wicked to sell a slave. Sometimes Brunehaut was so sweet it hurt Valrada's teeth to listen to her.

The new beads glittered in the sunlight. Freed, then. Anything to get the whore off Poijou.

She could be given to the church. Brunehaut would consent to *that*. Valrada almost smiled. When Rikimer returned, Domnola would be gone.

Leaving the women at the river, Valrada found herself turning to the mews instead of the Hall.

Berto's falcon was molting; she hunched on her block in the sunny south yard.

There was no need for *her* to fall to Rikimer. Were Brunehaut's baby not to be a boy, Valrada vowed silently, she personally would free Berto's falcon.

Werner the mewskeeper sat in the mews doorway, snipping a merlin hood out of a skin. Valrada picked up a goose quill and began to scratch the falcon's feet. "Could she fend for herself if she escaped now?" she asked Werner innocently.

"Yes."

The falcon rattled her feathers and began to scratch her chin with one wicked talon.

A tremor at the edge of Valrada's sight turned into Antonia, rounding the corner of the mews.

"I've been at the Hall, *mea Domina*."

Antonia's usually jaunty voice was flat. Suddenly Valrada's heartbeats began to hurt. "Lady Brunehaut?"

"Couldn't be better." The assurance was spoken so heartily it sounded like a lie.

"Keep away from the bird," Werner snapped.

Meeting the falcon's baleful glare the midwife blenched and stumbled backward. Valrada's chin went up. The bird hadn't been that close. She made Werner give up his stool to Antonia, just to remind him whose mews these were. Antonia sat as if winded.

"Are you sure nothing's wrong with Lady Brunehaut?"

"Lady Brunehaut is in perfect health, stronger than I ever saw a woman at her time. And I've been thinking, *mea Domina*. If you really want to make certain you get a little brother, Lady Brunehaut should go to Poitiers."

Valrada habitually thought of Brunehaut's child as her nephew, or, God forbid, niece. She was so startled to hear it referred to as her brother that her mind took a moment to register the rest of Antonia's sentence. *"Go to Poitiers?"*

"St. Hilary is very powerful, *mea Domina*, the most powerful saint in Gaul. Let Lady Brunehaut pray at his tomb and her child will certainly be male."

"It's too late," Valrada stammered. "She'd never make it to Poitiers. Her child would be born on the road."

"Oh, no, no, *mea Domina*, believe me, I've caught babies for thirty years and Lady Brunehaut can easily ride to Poitiers in time.

"Let her pray at St. Hilary's tomb, then enlist the prayers of the holy Radegonda, and you'll surely have a brother. And a baby born at the Convent of the Holy Cross carries a special blessing all its life, *mea Domina*. Your——"

"Lady Brunehaut cannot give birth in Ste. Croix," Valrada tried to speak slowly and think fast. "Doctor Nicolaus would not be permitted to attend her there."

"I'll attend her, *mea Domina*, and he'll never be missed.

Greeks don't know anything about babies we Romans don't know. The whole world over, they all get in and out the same way."

"Nicolaus has told me that in Constantinople——"

"Oh, in Constantinople babies are born with tails and you need a doctor to whack them off right away, but here in Gaul we've no need of Greek surgery."

"That will do, Antonia. If you have no more duties at the Hall, you may go home."

Valrada had no intention of burying herself in a convent now that Alarik was almost headed home at last. What suddenly ailed Antonia, talking such nonsense at this late date? Poor old soul, dread of what would happen if the baby were a girl had put her into a panic; she would have to be coaxed out of it. But for the moment, her impertinence had left Valrada with no patience for the task.

"Brunehaut's child will be born before autumn," she had reminded Alarik.

His sober face had grown graver still. "If it is a girl——"

"It won't be!"

"If it is, you should take refuge in Ste. Croix the day you hear the prince has been christened. Try to get Brunehaut to go with you. When I have your uncle's consent to our marriage, I'll come for you."

"And if he never consents?"

"Trust me; I'll come for you."

Only if Brunehaut's baby was a girl would Valrada set foot off Poijou, and after all God had asked Poijou to bear since the Year of Grace 580, He could not be planning to send its dead lord a daughter.

July 7, 585

DOMNOLA, ASLEEP ON THE STRAW SHE HAD SPREAD ON BRUNE-
haut's hearth, turned over. Brunehaut envied her.
The baby was stretching with all his might, which was
not small. It couldn't possibly be a girl, whatever Greek
Nicolaus said.

There really was nothing Brunehaut didn't dislike
about Nicolaus, from his greasy curls, his beard and
mustache so trimmed and plucked he must spend half his
life in front of a mirror, to, above all, his perfumed
hankerchief. For the past nine months, Brunehaut had
found Nicolaus's scent suffocating.

Two weeks ago, there'd been some improvement: He
had suddenly exchanged his perfume-soaked fillet for a
gold one.

Had Brunehaut ever commented on his fillet to
Valrada, they were to agree that fall, Valrada might have
thought to speak to her of the new gold beads that had
been twinkling on Domnola's wooden necklace those
same two weeks.

Such an exchange would have made a difference to
everyone on Poijou.

The child was still at last; Brunehaut slipped her feet
into shoes and shuffled to the window.

The air was no cooler without than within, and her son
was rebelling at his cramped space again. (Antonia
assured her he was an unusually big baby. Even Nicolaus
said so, too—again and again.)

The pressure under Brunehaut's ribs grew steadily
worse. Standing was no better than lying. Brunehaut was

dizzy. What if she fell? "Domnola." The summons came out a whisper and the girl didn't stir. Brunehaut's breath was so labored the girl must be dead not to waken. Ahh, but the baby was stopping. Ahhhhh. . . . Brunehaut shuffled back to the bed and managed to lie down.

She would call him Harrarik.

A new pressure distracted her; Domnola might have to be wakened after all. The chamber pot was under the bed, and Brunehaut wasn't sure she could get it. She turned laboriously from her back onto her side, feeling more urgency with each second. Gasping, she made it to the floor, to her knees. She hadn't started soon enough. The old mortifying crisis of early childhood: She felt herself bearing down, ready or not. "Domnola!" At last the pot was in her hand. She flung it across the room toward the sleeping girl.

As Domnola sat up, there was a ringing crack and her mistress began to scream for her god. For a thrilled moment, Domnola thought the sacred oak outside the window had crashed through the wall and fallen across the Christian's bed, but the room was intact, and Lady Brunehaut was upright on her knees. "The baby," Brunehaut screamed.

"What's the matter?" Valrada burst into the room.

"The waters have broken, my lady."

"Get Antonia."

Valrada helped Brunehaut onto the bed. Grasping her hand, Brunehaut gripped it until Valrada thought Alarik's ring would cut off her finger. "Don't tense," she urged. "Antonia said, let your muscles rule." When that contraction ended, Valrada took her hand away and gave Brunehaut the ringless one.

Warily, Brunehaut opened her eyes.

Valrada was praying, her eyes clenched. *I'm dying,*

Brunehaut realized. "Mother!" she sobbed. Valrada's frantic lips moved faster. "The priest!" Brunehaut cried. If she died before the baby came, he would die, too. "Knife, get a knife!" Antonia opened the door. "Save the baby!" Brunehaut cried. There was a long basket full of linens on Antonia's arm. On top lay a dark flask. Antonia set the basket down carefully against the wall. "Drink," she commanded, holding the flask to Brunehaut's lips.

Groaning, Brunehaut managed to turn her face away. Antonia laid her empty hand just below Brunehaut's ribs. In a minute Valrada saw the muscle under Antonia's hand go slack. "Now drink," Antonia ordered.

"Shall I go for Nicolaus?" Valrada whispered.

"Domnola's gone." Brunehaut's hands were no longer clawing at the sheets. "*She's* all right," Antonia jerked her head at Brunehaut. "Do you want to show him your knees?"

Valrada suddenly remembered she was dressed only in her shift.

"Get along with you," said Antonia.

Valrada sat on the edge of her clothes chest. It helped that Brunehaut was no longer moaning. Yet the silence seemed awful.

Domnola and Nicolaus had hurried up the stairs and gone into Brunehaut's room what seemed ages ago, and though Valrada's door was open, she'd heard nothing since. Several times she'd gone to her door and once partway down the hall, but she couldn't persuade herself to go back to Brunehaut's room. She didn't admit to any squeamishness about blood. Brunehaut had never been exposed to her; she would be mortified, and not just that Valrada was seeing her half naked, but that she was seeing her half naked in front of Nicolaus. In fact, Valrada couldn't face it herself. She hunched on her bed.

A small but furious yell pierced the silence and Valrada was across the room before she knew she was on her feet. She hovered in the hall waiting for Brunehaut's door to open, for Antonia to beckon. Was it male?

No one came. The baby's cries ceased. That was good, wasn't it? Youngest of her family, Valrada knew nothing. Did the baby's cries trail off like that because he was nursing—or what? Why didn't that fiend Antonia send Domnola to tell her how things stood?

Brunehaut wouldn't nurse her child with Nicolaus there.

Everything was too quiet. Valrada began to creep down the hall.

"Antonia!"

The midwife started. She was emerging from Brunehaut's room, her long basket over her arm, Domnola close behind with a lamp. For a moment Antonia stood frowning at Valrada, then abruptly transferred her basket to Domnola's free arm. "Take these rags and burn them," she muttered. Domnola looked anything but pleased, and as she took the basket her arm sagged to dramatize its weight, which couldn't have been notable. Domnola always dramatized how much was demanded of her. Antonia's eyes flashed at Domnola's hesitation, and with a last furtive glance at Valrada the girl proceeded down the stairs alone. Antonia took Valrada by the arm and led her back down the hall to her own room.

There was nothing in the least wrong with Brunehaut, but she still slept from the drink Antonia had given her. The baby, however, was a girl.

Valrada sank down on her bed.

Rikimer had won.

What would become of them?

"You must tell her, *mea Domina*."

"I!"

"It's a beautiful, healthy girl. You'll love——"

"Tell her yourself." Antonia's eyes turned inward. "What about Nicolaus?" Valrada tried.

Antonia appeared to be talking to the border of Valrada's tunic. "Lady Brunehaut and her baby are in excellent condition, *mea Domina,* and Nicolaus says— Nicolaus says he may not speak to Lady Brunehaut again until she has been purified from childbirth."

"What are you talking about? Nicolaus says! *Nicolaus* says he *may not*——"

"It's his religion, *mea Domina*."

"Well, it's not ours! I never heard anything so outrageous. Did he never see my mother between childbed and church? That's preposterous; my father never would have stood for it. This Greek. . . ."

Antonia bore Valrada's words as if they were blows— but mulelike, neither dodging nor responding. Valrada took a deep breath.

Did Nicolaus think he could begin to indulge himself the minute Brunehaut had a daughter? Valrada couldn't understand why Antonia wasn't equally hot. She just slumped there looking, Valrada conceded remorsefully, old and unsure. *She knows how her life will change when my dear cousin is Poijou's lord.*

So nobody could face Brunehaut with the bad news. Well, maybe Brunehaut would prefer it from Valrada.

Nicolaus was standing by the window looking eastward at the reddening clouds. Valrada felt a moment's resentment of the sun for rising not an hour later than normal, and she felt another at the doctor's back. He generally wasted her time with too many flourishes.

Brunehaut was still sleeping, and the baby lay in its cradle. On Valrada's command, Antonia moved one candle so that Valrada could see the sleeping child.

Only the small head showed, for the baby was swaddled. Against the white linen its skin was dark, its cheeks a deep rose. Valrada was astonished at its appeal. She had seen new babies before; they were all ugly. Did it actually make a difference, that this one was her—was Brunehaut's? She blinked hard against a sudden stinging in her eyes, started to touch the child, sleeping or no, then abruptly remembered the two avid aliens and straightened up. "What a lot," she observed, "of hair she has."

Antonia snuffed the candle. "You were born just so." Valrada looked at the soundly sleeping baby, whose head was covered with black waves. "Those are birth locks," Antonia said. "They'll all come out. By the time she's a year old she'll be a tow head, like her mother." The door opened and Domnola reentered. At a curt gesture from Antonia she began to extinguish the remaining candles.

Brunehaut stirred and Nicolaus, who had hung back all this while, suddenly thrust forward. "Your indulgence, gracious lady." He bowed over Valrada's hand as deeply as ever but with considerably more dispatch. Valrada looked down distastefully at the sleek, pomaded curls. The first entering rays of the sun winked at her from the Greek doctor's new gold fillet.

As the door closed behind Nicolaus, Valrada also wanted to escape, but she placed herself by the head of Brunehaut's bed. How old Brunehaut looked! In the shadows, her fair face was colorless and actually lined, and her long blond hair was matted and tangled like a senile peasant's. The blue eyes opened, and they, at least, were the same.

"Brunehaut," Valrada whispered.

Brunehaut looked at her.

"Brunehaut," Valrada said, a little louder and faster, "you have a beautiful daughter. Everything's fine. You——"

Brunehaut smiled sweetly. "Where is she?"

Valrada stared. Then she turned with a great rush of relief. Antonia had followed Nicolaus out of the room and the two were still muttering at each other in the hall, so Valrada nodded to Domnola to bring the baby.

As Domnola bent over Brunehaut's child the first sunlight invaded the corner where the cradle stood. It struck Domnola's necklace, glancing weakly from the iron cross, darkening each tiny wooden sphere with the next one's shadow. Among them the slave girl's two new golden beads glared at Valrada like eyes. Valrada's "No!" sounded like a flat hand smacking water. Domnola froze. "I'll do it," Valrada added quietly.

She wouldn't have reacted that way, she supposed, had the baby been a boy, but to see Brunehaut's daughter handled by Rikimer's whore revolted her.

She laid the linen cocoon beside Brunehaut. With a white finger Brunehaut brushed a lock of soft black hair back from the sleeping baby's forehead. Brunehaut's smile had grown, a new smile that shut Valrada out. "We'll name her Ingund," she murmured. "Maybe it will give her luck." Ingund, it slowly dawned on Valrada, had been one of the six royal wives of little Prince Clotar's grandfather, old Clotar I. Now Brunehaut included Valrada in her smile. "Maybe she'll grow up to marry a King Clotar, too."

With this pleasantry—which something told Valrada

was more than half in perfect earnest—Brunehaut closed her eyes again.

 XXII

July 14, 585

THE FOREST WAS ALREADY DARK. ANTONIA KNEW HER PATH, surely, but she stumbled over something. A branch must have fallen since last time. She held her burden closer and felt her way more slowly. The smell of centuries of rot surrounded her, drowning her. She walked on, peering as through water. In her mind, she saw herself resting waterlogged on the forest floor, the burden in her arms slowly detached from her lifeless arms, slowly floating back past her hut, through the village, up to Poijou Hall; bobbing on the surface, caught now and then by something—an apple tree, a shed corner—but always washed free and borne slowly on until it came to rest, ducking and rising gently on the waves of thick warm forest air, bumping at the door of the Hall. Her mouth was sticky and tasted of salt.

The tree frogs fell silent as she advanced. Something scuttled away, from quite nearby. Trees closed together around her, the alien, isolating her, condemning. The trees leaned over her as if they debated whether to bend altogether and crush her.

Going home there would be still less light. They always came on moonless nights.

knew what she had done, she was anything but sorry to see the bird returned. Too late, Werner mewskeeper's rage and desolation had made her realize that the vanished falcon had never been Berto's, but Werner's, and that it could never have been Rikimer's, either, but always, only, Werner's. She had acted before she analyzed, and caused grief....

The old woman spoke to her retinue in a rapid, singing language Valrada had never heard, and Valrada noticed the Poijou women all cross themselves. The boy and the two young women set off toward the mews. None of them had opened his mouth. Valrada tried not to wonder about their teeth.

The old woman's were gleaming white; she sucked their little points as Valrada took some coins out of her purse. "Werner is to give the boy these," Valrada told one of Poijou's slaves.

The slave took the money reluctantly, then stood looking at her feet.

Valrada didn't want these strangers on Poijou unescorted. "Agnes, you go with her," she ordered one of the other wide-eyed Romans. Agnes and the woman with the money exchanged an eloquent look and set out close together after the silent trio.

Under the willow, Domnola set up folding stools. "Liguria," the ancient visitor announced softly. Then she folded her hands in her lap and waited for Valrada to speak.

Valrada had a curious feeling that if she gave the old woman her name, the old woman would keep it. "The falcon was my brother's. I thank you for returning her."

The woman who called herself Liguria (at least to Valrada) kept her black eyes persistently, almost insolently, working Valrada's face. "Hair like the beech in October is not given to many," she murmured. "Has your brother also this gift?"

Valrada felt an urgent reluctance to answer anything about Berto, as if to do so would imperil his soul.

Liguria stared at the amethyst in Valrada's headband. "Was it your brother gave you the grapestone?"

From the sly way she asked, Valrada was sure the creature believed it was a lover's gift. "The stone was a present from my godmother." Valrada stressed *god* as if the word were a defensive weapon.

"There has been someone who has given you gifts who stood in no relation to you," Liguria observed. Alarik's ring burned Valrada's finger. A thin white scar ran from the corner of the strange visitor's mouth to just below her left eye, making the eye squint when she spoke. She squinted at Valrada's face. "Sometimes the greatest gift we are given, we cannot keep."

Valrada returned her almost insulting stare. The remark had an edge, obviously expected to cut, but she had never received anything too embarrassing to keep.

Liguria frowned pointedly at Domnola, who had remained close. "I have a gift that can be shared or kept," she told Valrada at last.

Perhaps the old woman was merely senile. Valrada glanced restlessly back at her neglected work and caught three of her women peeking at her over their tenter frames. They ducked at once, but she knew as well as if she had the gift of sight that behind their woolen webs the women were all whispering, not working.

"It is the gift of sight."

Valrada gasped. Had the woman read her mind? No, but she was offering....

She was offering to lead Valrada into mortal sin.

"Your hand is surely too white to have much written on it," Liguria suggested, as if, Valrada thought, she believed just the opposite.

All Valrada's hungry questions clamored like fledglings. Was Alarik safe? Did he truly love her? Would they marry?

Would she live to see her cousin smashed?

In place of a collar the ancient stranger wore a necklace of amber. The biggest bead contained a petrified bee: The necklace looked like honey bewitched. "All things are in the hand," she murmured, "the hidden things of darkness, the counsels of the heart."

Consulting a soothsayer was a mortal sin, leading straight to hell—but not if the sinner repented! Valrada knew she would repent, especially if she heard something she didn't like.

The river flowed by with a seductive, scarcely audible murmur. Through the green silk screen of drooping willow branches the waterlilies looked like floating candles. A dragonfly on shimmering wings trembled near Valrada's knee for an instant, then shot away. Was so much loveliness to pass to Rikimer, the murderer?

"Go help with the webs," Valrada ordered Domnola.

On tenterhooks herself, now, Valrada put out her hand.

"Those who need a lamp's light, pour in oil."

Valrada snatched back her hand. Taking a coin from her purse, she bent to give it as surreptitiously as possible.

"A lady ties her purse with spiderweb," Liguria grumbled. Yet it wasn't a small coin.

Again Valrada placed her hand palm upward on her

knee. "When," she demanded, pressing her knees together so they couldn't tremble, "shall I marry?"

Was it triumph or amusement that gleamed in the hard black eyes? The question, Valrada sensed, was exactly the one she had been expected to ask. She was cold all over. The old woman's fingers, sliding under hers, felt warm and dry.

Liguria studied the lines in the slender hand, not failing to note the marks left by a ring only very recently slipped off. "You will marry," she said slowly, "but there will be no Morning Gift."

She seemed to wait for Valrada's reaction, but Valrada continued to sit, her free hand clenched till its knuckles whitened, her eyes glued to her open hand as if she could read it herself. *When?*

"No Morning Gift," Liguria repeated ominously, "for the bride whose joy has come too soon."

Later, Valrada could not imagine why it had not been clear to her what "joy" the old woman meant, but at the time her only thought was that if the old woman saw signs of a negligible Morning Gift, it was a good omen, indicating that Valrada's uncle was going to consent to her marriage to a poor man.

Liguria's voice deepened. "Bad, very bad," she muttered, shaking her head over Valrada's palm, then looking up to see how Valrada was taking it. Liguria had never seen a girl accept so coolly the warning that there would be no virginity price. "Time will explain all," she warned hatefully.

Valrada began to feel, not shaken, as Liguria intended, but impatient. Then she thought she realized what the matter was, and with her left hand, fumbled for her purse.

Liguria's teeth shone. She had begun to be afraid that the brother this girl spoke of was the child's father. If the bastard got its looks from its father, there would be no finding the mother. But no, the girl was paying. "The most prized gift makes the most prized gift," Liguria said, looking pointedly at Valrada's amethyst.

Suddenly Valrada felt weary. Whatever the old woman's powers of seeing what was to come, she couldn't make things come sooner, or differently. Valrada would have thrown her chaplet into the river to bring Alarik home a month before it was now ordained that he should come, but whenever that was, he would come then and not sooner. This old woman couldn't alter it.

Liguria saw the change in Valrada's eyes and felt it in her hand. Hastily she lifted the hand a little nearer to herself. "You have been most foully harmed by one you had reason to trust." Along the edges of Valrada's upturned forearm the fine hairs rose. "A man. You have been betrayed. You have been brought almost to ruin. Perhaps you will be ruined yet," Liguria took care to say, "because of this man."

"Yes," Valrada whispered; "Yes."

Liguria let their hands fall back in Valrada's lap. "It is better to avenge than to mourn."

Valrada's heart began to pound.

Liguria withdrew her hand and reached into the neck of her tunic, bringing forth a small furry bag that hung from a thong which the tunic concealed. She laid the bag in her lap. "The judge is condemned when the criminal is left free." She had never encountered an unmarried mother so difficult to blackmail, but once a murderess, this cool redhead would be hers.

Valrada scarcely breathed. Outside the willow's shade

the heat shimmered. Through its waves the swallows that darted about the sky, the women working at the frames, looked far away, unreal. No sound came from them to Valrada. The world under the willow was dark and secret. Valrada knew what the bag held.

"What is this?"

At their distance Antonia's words weren't distinct enough to be understood by the two women under the tree, but her angry scream broke the surface of their silence as the osprey shatters smooth water. With a shiver Valrada rose, looked once at Liguria as if she couldn't believe the old woman sat there, and stepped out into the sunlight.

Across the field, Antonia and Brunehaut, with Ingund, were confronting the three strangers returning from the mews. Brunehaut, clutching Ingund, turned and retreated for home. Valrada couldn't hear Antonia's tirade, but she saw Antonia's arm fling out. The boy and his mute companions hurriedly changed their direction to the one in which Antonia pointed—toward the road.

Then Liguria followed Valrada out from under the willow, and Antonia saw her.

For a moment Antonia stood very still. Then she charged.

Liguria watched her come. The poison bag had already disappeared. Once the red mouth grinned, showing the tips of pointed teeth, but Liguria's face was impassive by the time Antonia reached the riverbank. Valrada unconsciously stepped back as the two women confronted each other.

"Your friends are waiting for you on the road," Antonia said.

Beside Liguria, the elderly midwife was a woman in her prime. She did and she did not give an impression of the greater strength. Like a sunset, what Valrada saw changed, from moment to moment, without any movement. One second Antonia was powerful in righteousness and Liguria was the intruder, frail and humble. The next second Antonia was vulnerable, baffled, and frustrated, as if Liguria stood on her own soil, timeless and all-weathering as a rock, and Antonia was the interloper.

"We came to do this Hall a service." Liguria's voice whined, but her eyes glittered.

"When frogs have hair."

"They have brought back—my brother's—falcon."

Neither woman looked at Valrada. "You are welcome where you came from," Antonia told Liguria.

"Don't snap your fingers at dogs, Roman, before you're out of their village."

Antonia spat.

Liguria left unhurriedly. Antonia rounded on Valrada. "Certainly you could see they were no Christians, *mea Domina*, with all those heathen beads and not a cross among the lot!" Valrada winced: Still unpurified from Ingund's birth, Brunehaut hadn't received the host for nearly forty days. "What was she buzzing to you under that tree? Phew! I wonder you could stand her stink! Have you still got your purse?"

"You used the poor creatures disgracefully. If they were thieves, they could have sold our falcon, not brought her back."

"They probably stole the bird to begin with. They should stick to poultry like the foxes they are. We decent people work hard, then along come such folk and expect to get what we've—but *I'll* not play badger to anybody's fox!"

Valrada understood the midwife's simile better than its application. Alarik had told her how the lazy fox often stole a good burrow: "The badger is the best digger of all animals. When a vixen finds a badger hole, she makes her stench at its mouth. The badger can't stand it. He moves out and she moves in."

But what had Liguria's party tried to take from Antonia? If they had foxed more money out of Valrada than was proper, it wasn't the midwife's money. "That will do, Antonia," Valrada said.

XXV

August 9, 585

IN THE COURTYARD THE TWO *RHEDA* HORSES DROOPED BETWEEN the shafts. The two pigeons Brunehaut was to offer at the church huddled in their basket inside the *rheda's* curtained darkness. Valrada climbed in beside Brunehaut, opposite Domnola and Ingund.

Brunehaut, Valrada knew, would have preferred to hold Ingund herself, but if Ingund smelled milk she would give no peace till she was fed, and it would be disastrous for Brunehaut to nurse her while wearing white silk.

Priest and congregation were waiting outside the church. Brunehaut let the priest come to her. The sudden change from dark to light as Domnola handed her down

from the *rheda* to Valrada had wakened Ingund: She
roared in Valrada's arms. A sigh exhaled from the crowd.
Valrada could see them wishing that such a strong child,
so lusty, could only be male. Just, she realized, as they
would rather she had been killed than her brother.

What if she were suddenly to rise in church some
Sunday this autumn and scream to them what Rikimer
had done...would they tear him apart? Then how
many—starting with herself—would die to pay for it?
She shook herself; the sun was getting to her.

The priest gave Brunehaut one end of his stole to hold
and, shouldering the wailing baby, led the way inside.

"O Christ, the True Light," the priest sang, leading
Brunehaut to light the candles on St. Genevieve's shrine.

"...that we may behold the unapproachable Light," the
congregation chanted as the little procession moved again
toward the altar.

At least the coolness of the church silenced Ingund.

An ivory box of sacred oil stood on the altar. The scene
adorning the side facing Brunehaut was St. Germanus
presenting the tiny Genevieve with the coin she was to
wear always, to remind her of her lisping promise to keep
her body untouched to the end. Overhead in the carved
clouds, angels of undeterminable sex rejoiced. "Let us
pray;" the priest returned the baby to her kneeling
mother. "Almighty God . . ." he made the sign of the cross
on Ingund's forehead with holy oil.

Behind them, Valrada was surprised at how quietly
Ingund bore this. Something else was distracting the
child. As Brunehaut had predicted, on being returned to
the accustomed region of her meals she was busily
rummaging with both hands and nose.

"...we beseech Thee," the priest traced a cross on

Brunehaut's forehead, "purify from sin and pollution this Thy handmaid..."

Ingund was beginning to fuss.

"...whom Thou has preserved..."

Ingund's frustration was increasing audibly and Valrada could see Brunehaut deliberately clasp her closer to the tantalizingly odorous bosom.

"...that she may be permitted to take, without condemnation, of Thy holy mysteries," the priest prayed.

The moment for Domnola to rise and present the priest the symbolic basket had come, and without turning her head, Valrada gave her the sign. The moment drew out. Valrada stole a sideways look. Domnola was frozen to the floor, on her face a look of terror-born stubbornness which Valrada had seen on horses that would die before letting themselves be put into unfamiliar stalls. Valrada sighed and made the presentation of the pigeons herself.

Now Brunehaut might take communion again with the others in spite of her motherhood. "Almighty God, from whom no secrets are hid..." the priest began the ancient entreaty. The wails of the baby in Brunehaut's arms rang through the church.

Brunehaut was first to descend when the *rheda* drew up at Poijou Hall. A man stepped out of the group of waiting servants.

"Lady, give me lodging and food," the minstrel said, "and God will bless your old age, and have compassion on him you have lost."

Brunehaut flinched backward, almost colliding with Valrada. Across the minstrel's bowed back Valrada saw Nicolaus's smirk. Song at the waiting feast was his gift:

The minstrel was wending his way south from Paris; Nicolaus knew their ladyships would wish to hear how it fared the Neustrians there, and their prince....

Inside the *rheda*, Domnola heard the minstrel's accent and shrank back, as shaken as if the *rheda* still moved. The man was Breton. Had Bel sent him to destroy her, or as a sign that she was forgiven?

She had had to let the Christian priest put his chalice to her lips, but not a drop had passed them. Domnola hadn't been so frightened since being dragged into this landlocked country. Then Cat-eyes had made her the sign! They hadn't told her she would be making an offering *at their altar*. "When I give you the sign," Cat-eyes had said, "you're to hand the priest the basket." Two stringy pigeons was hardly an offering Bel would be jealous of. Domnola had felt safe accepting Cat-eyes' order; she'd actually had to conceal a smile of contempt.

If she'd known they meant right at their altar, she wouldn't have set foot toward the church. She'd have feigned illness; she could have stolen a chicken and used its blood.

Valrada stood numbly. "...him you have lost." It was her brother, dying unshriven in the forest, whom she had seen in the brief light the minstrel's words had flashed on the curtained-off places of her mind. Then she remembered her father's death.

The war was over; Alarik and her uncle were safe, she told herself.

That there was yet another *him* she might have lost, she never guessed.

In the *rheda*, Ingund whimpered. Valrada passed her hand over her eyes and turned to take the baby so Domnola could climb down. One of the *rheda*'s curtains brushed Ingund's cap off. The minstrel had retrieved it in an instant. As he gave the little cap to Valrada, his black eyes looked so intently at the child on her shoulder that Brunehaut snatched Ingund into her own arms. "Take him to the kitchen," she ordered Domnola.

The babble in the courtyard was behind them. Nothing moved but the two of them and the shimmering heat. They were nearly at the back of the Hall and still the bard was silent. Domnola stopped. "Have you nothing to say to me?" She spoke Breton.

"You're in danger."

Domnola's vision blurred and her heart began to pound.

"It is the flawed vessel that cracks."

Where was she flawed?

The minstrel regarded her steadily. "Leave this place for the first reason offered."

She felt hot between the legs. If he meant that small tear, he could go to hell.

The minstrel shrugged. "As you've arranged the thread, so you must weave it."

A spit-boy chasing a dog with a chicken leg in its jaws tore around the corner of the Hall and almost knocked Domnola off her feet, and the minstrel passed into the kitchen.

"I sing to Prince Clotar, who will be lifted on the shield Monday next." The minstrel paused to give the reaction of the long table time to quiet. "The anthem of his grandfathers."

Victory! Our fathers fell in battle. . . .

Valrada sat staring at her plate. If the shielding was Monday next, Rikimer and her uncle would be home before Harvest Moon. It was time for her and Brunehaut to go to Ste. Croix.

"Riddle me this," cried the minstrel:

Silver is the sea in the light of the moon;
Gold are the hills in the light of the sun,
But the red star that shines in the forest
Lights no one.

The sun is the father of the moon,
The moon is the daughter of the sun,
But the red star that shines in the forest
Has no one.

Valrada's hand, the hand in which the old woman had pretended to see her future, began, she could not have said why, to tremble. She managed to keep her voice steady. "Explain this 'star' for us, minstrel."

"Lady, I do not know yet what it will mean—but I believe we shall both know by All Saints' Day." The minstrel began to strum his harp again before Valrada could say another word.

I saw no moonlight this full moon
For the brightness of a fire:
I saw a child in his nurse's arms
With hair like a beacon pyre.

Like a torch his hair was blazing
Till it set the roof aflame:
His nurse's hut burnt to the ground
But the babe's hair blazed the same.

And all around was ashes,
And all around was night,
And all around was sorrow,
But the babe's hair still burned bright.

Halfway down the table Antonia doubled over, choking. Later—about two months later—Valrada and Brunehaut both remembered how she quickly held up a fishbone she said had lodged in her throat.

Antonia was to remember the ashes.

XXVI

August 585

"WE COULD AT LEAST GIVE THE LITTLE BITCH TO THE CHURCH," Valrada urged.

"Takes too long," Brunehaut answered. "Too many papers."

Valrada, reflecting that Rikimer would only buy Domnola back if he wanted her, said no more.

"Lady Brunehaut and I are going on pilgrimage," she told Poijou's priest, "to pray at my father's tomb." Two days after the minstrel had come and gone, Brunehaut and Valrada attached their *rheda* and cart to an oil merchant's caravan.

At dawn of the last day of that broiling week, Valrada could distinguish the Basilica of St. Hilary's, where her father's body lay. The sanctuary's cross gleamed like a beacon against Poitiers' high southern gate.

A subdeacon led Valrada to the grave. There were fresh asters on Lord Eurik's stone—for which the subdeacon had no explanation.

Brunehaut had elected to do her praying at St. Hilary's tomb, which in addition to its reputation for miracles, was inside a cool chapel. Valrada knelt beside her father's grave.

Brunehaut was already waiting in the *rheda* when she stood up.

"Hard by the far walls," the subdeacon said, pointing northeast as if Poitiers' bulwarks were transparent and Valrada could see the Convent of the Holy Cross by sighting along his finger. "Past the Jewish quarter. Anyone can tell you."

Valrada stared straight ahead. Brunehaut leaned through the parted curtains, telling Ingund what she saw as if the infant were her blind, senile grandmother. "An apple orchard, right between those great big houses," she breathed. "Oh, what a pretty vineyard! Big blue grapes. Wouldn't you like a big blue grape?" Valrada wanted to scream.

The convent walls were high and strong. "No one," said Brunehaut, her Mummy-voice put aside, thank God, as last, "will remove us from this place against our desire."

And with their desire? Less than a week of Abbess Agnes's protection taught Valrada how Berto's falcon felt, chained to her perch, day after day after day.

Brunehaut and Valrada, as temporary refugees, were not required to cook or sweep or carry wood, but they rose to pray before dawn, they were read the disquisitions of St. Augustine at breakfast, they were read the Gospels as they sewed all morning, as they ate midday broth, as they sewed all afternoon. The abbess, a Roman, was conspicuously disappointed that neither could read. Valrada bristled to ask her who had freed Poitiers from the heretics, Frankish heroes or Roman clerks? Brunehaut only held Ingund closer and smiled.

Relieved of all the cares of Poijou, Ingund shared with no one and admired by everyone, Brunehaut sat at her spinning, rocking Ingund's cradle with one foot, dreamily oblivious of the everlasting Latin drumming at them from the middle of the room. Valrada half expected her to stand and disclose that she had hatched another Ingund under her skirts.

"Judge nothing before the time, until the Lord come, who will bring to light the hid—" The sister stopped reading in midword as Mother Agnes appeared.

"Someones wishes to see you," Mother Agnes told Valrada. The tatting slithered from Valrada's lap as she started forward. The abbess looked at it. Valrada stopped in midstep, picked up the wretched scrap, and dropped it behind her on her stool. "Sister Stella will escort you," the abbess said, and left.

Valrada fought the impulse to sling the stool at the back of Mother Agnes's head, but the promised guest was surely Alarik, and in scarcely the time it took to exchange a look with Brunehaut, Valrada was across the room to the door where Sister Stella waited.

It was a piece of meanness in that atrophied Roman

abbess to give her for a guide Sister Stella, who had taken a vow of silence. Sister Stella led Valrada to the doorway to the herb garden, opened it, and left.

There was no one in the little walled garden but a novice kneeling at prayer before the cross in the far corner. Sister Stella must have gone to fetch Alarik. The novice would be there for chaperone. Let her keep praying, or she'd wish she had.

Valrada walked to one of the benches but couldn't sit. She could hear no approaching steps—nothing but the bees droning in the roses. That novice was peeping already. Let her turn her head once more and Valrada would twist it off.

"Mea Domina." The novice was on her knees in front of Valrada. "Pardon!"

In seven months, Claudia's face had grown sallow. Otherwise, cocooned as she was from crown to instep, what could Valrada tell?

Claudia wrung her hands. "I asked to see you, *mea Domina,* because——"

"You asked to see me!"

Claudia's mouth worked.

"So *you* are my guest?"

"I had to run away, *mea Domina.* I didn't want to. I loved Poijou. I loved——"

"You loved a young man."

Claudia hung her head.

"Well, what happened to him?"

Claudia shrugged.

"You haven't been here all seven months, have you?"

"No, *mea Domina,"* Claudia whispered. "Only one."

"Where were you before?"

"At Poijou, *mea Domina."*

Valrada sat down.

"Antonia hid me until—I could travel."

Valrada pondered the top of Claudia's head. "And what did become," Valrada asked gently this time, "of your young man?"

"He died fighting the Pretender at Convenae."

"I'm sorry."

"He deserved to die!"

The sweetest wine made the sharpest vinegar. . . . "And the child?"

"Antonia sent it to her daughter in Bordeaux."

"You never did have a sister, did you, Claudia?"

"No, *mea Domina.*"

"Well, get up; I'm not your mistress now. Tell Lady Brunehaut your story." *And hurry up about it. She won't be Lady of Poijou much longer.*

"You tell her, *mea Domina.* Lady Brunehaut isn't—Lady Brunehaut is—you've known Poijou's folk all your life, you've known me——"

"I've known you so well I didn't know you had no sister."

Claudia began to weep. "I can't stand this life, *mea Domina.* Tell Lady Brunehaut to take me back; I can't be a nun! I——"

"Oh, you'll never be satisfied. At Poijou you sulked because you were a servant. Here you can be sister to three kings' daughters—and you're wailing."

"I might as well still be a floor scrubber! We're always praying, praying—my knees are hard as a camel's. What do I care about kings' daughters? Sister Radegonda is *old,* and those other two are ugly bi— aren't near as pretty as you, *mea Domina.*"

"I look as I looked seven months ago."

Claudia sobbed. "If your lady mother were alive...I

pray for your mother every day, *mea Domina*. I put flowers on your father's grave every Sunday." At the change in Valrada's expression, Claudia's tears diminished. "It's the only time they ever let me out of these walls. And then they always send some sister with me." She began to cry again.

Valrada sighed. "Lady Brunehaut and I will speak to Mother Agnes about you."

Claudia's tears ceased abruptly. "Speak to Sister Radegonda. She made Mother Agnes abbess. Mother Agnes does what she says."

XXVII

September 17, 585

ONE YEAR AGO TODAY RIKIMER HAD SAT at THIS TABLE considering the offer of his cousin's hand. Then his place had been with the deacon, across the desk, where the deacon sat now, alone. Rikimer leaned back in his chair. There was no reason to think of it as his uncle's chair. Eurik had never been any more entitled to Poijou than Rikimer's father. Eurik had taken the best of their father's holdings simply because Dag was a coward.

The view from the window wasn't the same as last September's. Rikimer was grateful for the night that hid the hillside's grapes, raisins on the vine under a sky from which no rain had fallen since July. Ploughshares bounced on the ground; yesterday four men had needed all morning to dig a grave for one old woman.

Rikimer hadn't shown himself at the funeral. Poijou's

brutes were muttering that the rains had ceased when Lady Brunehaut left.

"My father," Rikimer told the deacon, "has received an interesting letter from the Abbess of Ste. Croix. My cousin Valrada wants to marry Alarik Alansson."

"*That* explains why our animal doctor insisted on switching his benefice from Poijou to Antier. Better your father's man than yours."

"She wants Poijou's priest as part of her dowry. Aside from this, if my father lets her marry Alarik, she'll accept any dowry my father thinks fair." Both men grinned. Valrada would have to do just that in any case.

"In conclusion, the Abbess further quotes her, my cousin 'will die in Ste. Croix' before she'll marry me."

"That, also, is up to your father. Unless the Abbess wants to support a penniless refugee for the rest of her life. Rare Abbess."

"And unless my mother gets wind of the letter. If she decides my father should give his consent to Valrada's becoming a nun—and you know she would—my father might give it."

The two men's gazes met. The Convent determined its novitiates' dowries, not the girls themselves, not their guardians. "Convents," observed the deacon, "aren't so easily satisfied as idiot girls who imagine themselves in love."

"Just so. I shall therefore encourage my father to give the lovers a big blessing and a *small* dowry—if, and only if, I can find myself another bride with a *larger* dowry. Otherwise, I continue to insist on Valrada for myself, damn my mother, damn Alarik Alansson, damn all."

"And who. . . ." The deacon, who knew very well who, allowed his voice to trail off.

"Lehun of Claigne *ought* to be glad to give me his daughter."

Rikimer looked out the window, frowning; the deacon resumed reading him his accounts.

"...which makes eight gold *solidi.*"

The deacon held up his scroll so that his sleeve fell back to his elbow. The deacon daily rubbed his forearms with pumice till they were as hairless as Domnola's belly. Rikimer knew what was sometimes whispered about himself and his deacon. He wondered if the slander had reached Lehun, whether that was why his overtures were being stalled off.

"My lord," the steward announced from the door, "Mark of Vien."

Mark's fields lay immediately south of Poijou. When the men had returned from Paris in late August, these fields had alternated red-gold wheat and paler barley. Now all were brown. Rikimer had been expecting Mark.

Mark had not been expecting the deacon. He bit his lip.

Rikimer poured Mark a cup of beer to give him time. On the desk beside the beer was a dish of pears, the season's finest, too meager to offer anyone. The beer was last year's.

"Toward Niort," Mark said, "they have fodder to sell."

"Some men keep that sort of useful news to themselves. You *are* a friend."

"They price their hay as if it were silk," Mark said.

"Perhaps you can barter some of your horses for it."

The deacon stroked his cross and looked at the scroll in his lap.

"We're bound to have rain!" Mark brought both fists down on the desk.

Mark's horses had eaten all his July cutting, meant to

last through December. "Horses will sell dear when King Gontram's quartermasters come through."

"Which will be?"

"Gontram plans to attack the Goths this month."

"What," Rikimer asked, "will our friends of Niort charge you for a month's fodder?"

Mark answered as if his mouth hurt.

Rikimer nodded and the deacon unlocked a little chest and counted out the sum Mark had named. "I must have some security," Rikimer said.

Mark took off his armlet.

"These are real garnets," Rikimer said.

Mark's lip curled, but he held his open purse at the edge of the table and pushed in the coins.

"I'll have to charge you two *deniers* a month for storing something so valuable. In advance."

Mark shrugged and loosened his purse strings again. Excommunication was for the one who charged interest, not for the one who paid.

The deacon entered Mark's loan.

"You have a very loyal servant." Mark did not quite sneer. Rikimer closed the door behind him and looked at the deacon. The deacon was wearing a handsome new gold enameled cross, double-bordered with pearls. It looked Byzantine. The deacon looked sleek. Rikimer wondered if he should have killed Mark.

If rumors got to his mother, she would chain herself in her chapel again.

His father would have let her starve and thanked God, only she had six brothers.

But for the drought, Rikimer had meant to begin calling on these uncles weeks ago. His father had brought home a mistress from the refugees from Convenae and installed her among Antier's weaving women. Rikimer's uncles didn't like him, but they'd do well to listen to him before the blonde southerner got a belly.

His uncles would have liked to see him fall at Convenae. If his father died sonless, Antier and Poijou would pass to them.

"My lord," the steward announced, "Luther of the Bourre."

Rikimer rose to strike hands, but Luther held out his arms to show that they were soot-coated. "I don't want to touch you."

"Fire."

"In my sheep pasture. We beat it out."

"Your sheep?"

"All safe; it blazed up about noon, and in this heat, I don't pasture them till sundown."

"We expected you last night," the deacon told Luther. "Your loan is past due."

"I need more time."

"I'd like to give it to you," Rikimer sighed, "but I lent you more than I can spare."

Luther untied his purse and turned it upside down. Nothing fell out.

The deacon tapped a tablet. "You made your mark here. Your land would attach to Poijou on September sixteenth if——"

"Surely," Luther urged Rikimer, "you can give me a little more time. I saved your life at Tours!"

"I was grateful, at Tours. You of all people should know that a mill can't grind with water that's past. The sum is more than I can afford to lose, and you cannot pay me. Your land is mine by right."

"But I? Am I to go? Where——"

"You know the answer," the deacon interrupted. "Bind yourself and you can farm your fields as if they were yours."

Luther stared at Rikimer. "Another month."

"A week."

The deacon looked after Luther thoughtfully. "Be careful," the deacon's grandmother had told him, the first time she'd seen Rikimer's knife-edge mouth. "There's one would pull meat from a funeral pyre."

The deacon's grandmother had been dotty for years. The first time she had seen him in his deacon's white vestment, his linen alb, she had jumped to the conclusion that he was a priest and nothing he could say could dissuade her. The deacon took this as an omen, but lately he was less anxious to see it proven. He wouldn't have cared to be in charge of that funeral yesterday. The people had been muttering; those who would look at him, looked ugly. The deacon had stolen away, and well-advised. Nicolaus had told him afterward that the widower had broken in on the priest's invocation. The rains had ceased, he shouted, the night the child was born that passed Poijou to Lord Rikimer's father. It was what they had all been whispering.

The priest had quieted them, but not easily. Nicolaus was as nervous as a chained dog that smells smoke. He wanted to go home to Constantinople.

"God be with you." Wulf Lehunsson had come upstairs unescorted. The deacon jumped to give Wulf his chair and pulled a bench up to the table for himself. Wulf stood pulling at the skin on his nose. Flat as it was, Wulf's nose was peeling.

The deacon had been surprised when Rikimer had

asked Lehun of Claigne's eldest son for security. Did he think he could get Wulf in deep enough to force that marriage contract?

Wulf cleared his throat.

"Your cows," Rikimer broached the subject for him, "are well."

Wulf glanced at the deacon. "Expensive to keep, of course." His voice, which he tried to make matter-of-fact, sounded congested. Wulf was always saying things designed to remind the deacon that his payments were for pasturing, certainly not for anything sinful like interest.

The door flew open and Rikimer's Breton burst in. "My lord! Nicolaus is dying!"

The deacon heard his bench crash onto its side and found himself on his feet.

"Stand still!" Rikimer rapped; after one moment's shocked fury the deacon realized he meant the girl. "Now, what's happened?"

Domnola glanced sideways at Wulf and the knowledge washed over the deacon that the slut was faking. "He's lying on the floor! There must have been fifty that got him! Ohhh!" she flung out her arms and swayed, but Rikimer didn't move. At once she steadied herself, dropping her hands to her face and moaning.

The deacon set his bench upright. His hands were trembling, but he would stake his life the bitch was faking. Wulf looked alarmed, but if he thought fifty peasants could break into Poijou Hall without the three of them hearing a shout, he was even more stupid than the deacon believed, which was impossible.

The steward appeared. "My lord, Nicolaus has been

severely stung. There appear to have been wasps in his lockchest. He wants us to submerge him, but do you wish us to use that much water——"

"No," Rikimer interrupted. The deacon's head jerked. "You," Rikimer told his wench, "get mud packs on him."

Rikimer turned to Wulf before the slut was out of the room. "Now what in hell were wasps doing in the man's chest?"

"He keeps honey in it." Instantly the deacon wished he'd held his tongue. Rikimer's gray eyes looked at him sharply and they seemed to see everything.

In the Convent of Ste. Croix, Valrada awakened clenched from a dream of a coppery meteor flashing through the sky over Poijou Hall to crash somewhere deep in the lightless forest. What had wakened her was the keening of a hundred foxes, but once she sat up she heard nothing but the snores of the twenty-three novitiates around her.

She lay back down. Closing her eyes brought, not sleep, but the unsettling memory of the minstrel who had stopped at Poijou in August on his way from where? to where? After his unanswered riddle, he had sung a strange song about a nurseling; her eyes had never left his as he sang, and for a moment, as his harp notes died, she had thought she was on the edge of an understanding that was vital. But the moment had passed like a melting snowflake.

She did not get back to sleep until morning, and she still did not know what she thought the dark minstrel had meant.

September 17, 585

THE GREEK'S OILED BODY WAS HELPLESS AND SLIMY AS A SNAIL jerked out of its shell. Domnola finished plastering mud on his stings and sat down with her back to him. What was Flat-nose here about? "You switch your tail around now," one of Poijou's cooks had told Domnola spitefully soon after Lord Rikimer had taken over, "but when Lord Lehun's daughter comes she'll beat it right off you." That was the first Domnola had heard of Flat-nose's sister.

Nicolaus moaned.

"Let Antonia nurse him," Domnola had protested, but Lord Rikimer had laughed.

"It's too hot for us anyhow," he'd said. Apparently if he didn't want to sleep with her, he didn't care whether or not she slept at all.

Nicolaus moaned again. "Give me a drink," he demanded.

Domnola gripped her candlestick in one hand, a half-filled cup in the other, and stamped over to the bed. She shoved the cup to Nicolaus's puffy lips, not quite daring to let candlewax drip on him. His whole body was swollen. The wasps must not have liked his smell; they had flown at him the moment he'd opened his chest and had hit everything before his screams brought help.

Domnola walked over to the window; lightning flashed, a grasping arthritic hand. "Give me a drink," Nicolaus groaned.

Domnola refilled his cup. He was getting Cat-eyes' bed plenty muddy—Domnola wished the fine lady were there to see it. She almost forgave the Greek for having preempted this room when that pair fled.

Nothing was exactly as Domnola had dreamed. She sank down again and her fingers moved to her throat. With the proper prayers to Bel she had thrown the cross that hung there into the river, so the drought couldn't be her fault.

The cross was gone from her string of beads, but all but two of the beads were still wooden. Lord Rikimer had promised, that first time, to change every one of them for gold.

That had been before the drought.

He would marry her when the drought broke, and she would have gold beads stitched all over her gown.

What about the Greek then, and Antonia? How much would she have to pay to keep them quiet? If only she had smothered the brat the moment she had it out of their sight! What had stopped her? Antonia and the Greek were afraid to kill it, afraid of their god, but Domnola didn't fear their god. Bel would have been pleased with the sacrifice of a Christian baby. *If He would just give her another chance. . . .*

What had Antonia *done* with the boy? Did the Greek know? Domnola had looked at every baby on Poijou. Where had Antonia hidden him?

Antonia wouldn't dare threaten her. Fear would keep the old hag quiet, whomever Lord Rikimer married; the Greek too. Domnola herself had thought briefly of telling Lord Rikimer about the manchild she had carried out of Lady Brunehaut's room to Antonia's hut, but she really did not think he would marry her to close her mouth. He was more likely to kill her.

"Give me a drink," Nicolaus whined.

Domnola stretched her string of amber full length and smiled to see the candlelight dance in each bead. This necklace was longer than the one the old lady had taken from her. Now that Domnola had the old lady's room she had searched every cranny without finding that one. These beads were a lighter color, the color of fox eyes. Domnola never took them off, not even to sleep. Lord Rikimer said they made her look all the more naked.

He wasn't like other Franks: about that much, she had been right. She grinned, remembering the steward's shock at finding Greek Nicolaus in nothing but his crucifix. Even in this heat, these Franks were all sleeping in their shifts.

"Beer," the Greek mouthed.

The door opened and the deacon stared at Domnola, sitting with her chair turned away from Nicolaus's bed fiddling with her heathen beads. "What are you doing? You were told to look after him!" He hurried to Nicolaus's side.

At the deacon's voice, Nicolaus began to whimper. "You bitch!" said the deacon.

"I'm dying," Nicolaus sniveled.

The lamp trembled in the deacon's hand. "You're not dying."

"Cut my hair like yours!"

Domnola held her head. If the Greek was going to be delirious, he would make more racket than ever.

"Tonsure me," Nicolaus caught at the deacon's sleeve. "Bring me one of your albs. I'm dying. I'll go to hell. Make me a priest. Hurry."

"You won't die." The deacon's voice was high. Nicolaus shook his sleeve. "I can't make you a priest!" The deacon seemed near tears. *"I'm* not a priest."

the door lest he kick her as he went by.

Antonia grinned derisively at his retreating back. "How's our fine *doctor?*"

Domnola shrugged and walked to the window. The vultures that for weeks had been as much a part of the sky as the sun, wheeled and circled.

"Sleeping," Antonia grunted. "I'm the one who needs sleep. I no more than lay down last night when Bella's man came running, in heat like this!"

Domnola lounged against the window, ostentatiously not listening.

"I took one look at Bella and told them both she was getting nowhere, but it was two hours before he would believe me and let me go home.

"Good God!" Antonia stared at Nicolaus.

Domnola leaped across the room. "Is he *dead?*"

"*What* is *this?*" Antonia bent and scooped up a handful of the Greek's shorn hair. "A priest, is it?" she whispered. "What does the fool think?"

Relief made Domnola tremble. It would be nothing to Bel if the Greek just died on his own.

Antonia threw the black curls back on the floor. "Sleeping like a stuffed flea on a fat dog and thinks he's dying. I'm the one should be in bed. The sun wasn't up before I was waked again, to come see *this*. Well, I've seen it." She loosened the strings of the bag hanging at her waist and took out a jar of palish unguent. "Rub that on him when the mud falls off. I'm going to bed."

Nicolaus was worse swollen than the night before. Domnola wondered if he would be able to open his eyes when he did waken. His Christian charm hung now over the back of the chair in which the deacon had spent the

night. Domnola tilted the chair so that the cross slid off
into the rushes.

"Ohhhh, Petros," moaned Nicolaus. Slits appeared in
the red-blue plums. "Ohhhh." He peered at Domnola.
"Thirsty!"

Domnola went for his cup. She paused long enough to
whisper the words over what she put into it, then took it
to him. Bel would prefer the knife, but she didn't dare.
"Drink this. It's medicine."

At the first taste, Nicolaus gagged and spit all over
himself. "You hellcat, what kind of poison are you giving
me?"

"It's medicine. The deacon left it for you."

Nicolaus inhaled and drank without breathing. When
the cup was empty he sank back gasping. Cup in hand,
Domnola stood watching him. His mouth twisted,
cleaning itself. She sat down, scarcely seeing the chair.
Her hand was sweating around the cup. She set the cup on
the floor and began to count her amber. She counted
slowly, silently, touching each bead, never taking her
eyes from the Greek's face.

"Ugh," Nicolaus shuddered. Domnola leaned forward.
"Unnhh." Domnola's heart beat faster and she let her
hand sink into her lap as another shudder shook Nicolaus
and he seemed to try to shift positions. The deacon's alb
slid to one side. Nicolaus began to breathe hard. His jaw
slackened so that his mouth stayed open; drool appeared
at its corners. Domnola's heart began to pound.

Nicolaus's breath came harder and harder and sweat
poured from his body. He began to groan. Domnola
picked up his cup, went quickly to the pitcher, poured a
little beer and carried the cup to the window. At the

sight of a cloud that was forming to the right of the sun
her heart almost left her chest. In the courtyard below
there was no one. Nothing moved but the great dark
birds high in the sky. Domnola sloshed the beer around
in Nicolaus's cup and emptied it out the window. The
beer hit the courtyard stones and steamed.

Nicolaus began to heave. When he succeeded in
bringing up something it choked him and he thrashed his
swollen arms and legs trying to raise himself. His teeth
were chattering. Suddenly he yelped. With an energy she
wouldn't have believed possible he got himself on his side
and, his head hanging over the edge of the bed, he
retched. Then he lifted his head. His eyes, red through
the slits in his swollen lids, met Domnola's.

Domnola turned her back. Across the hazy sky
lightning darted, quick as a snake's tongue. A low rumble
of thunder answered from far away. The vultures never
paused in their wheeling. Nicolaus heaved again. Then he
fell back, hands tearing at his stomach. Suddenly he
threw out his arms and his body began to bounce as if the
mattress were a roasting pan. Yell after yell tore out of
his tight purple face. His upper torso landed on one
shoulder on the floor; still his arms and legs thrashed.
Domnola heard running in the hall and hurried to
Nicolaus's side.

The deacon burst into the room, followed by Lord
Rikimer. The deacon screamed. Domnola got out of his
way.

The deacon had to dodge the Greek's flailing arms, but
he kept trying to take hold of Nicolaus. The steward and
several servants jammed the doorway, but Lord Rikimer
waved them back.

When Nicolaus finally stopped yelling the deacon rocked

back on his knees. "No, don't," he whimpered. "No, don't."
The dead body looked like a sausage.

The deacon was trying to lift it. Lord Rikimer moved in to help, but the deacon knocked his arm away. He got Nicolaus onto the bed and rounded on Domnola. "You *bitch,* why didn't you call me?"

Nicolaus's toes were splayed rigid, his mouth and eyes were open. Lord Rikimer picked up the soiled alb and put it over Nicolaus, covering his face.

"Hypocrite!" the deacon screamed.

Rikimer glanced at the door. Domnola went and shut it in the face of the lot of them, huddled in the hall like sheep at a barn-burning.

"It's your fault," the deacon sobbed. "He should have been put in cold water! He knew it, he *begged* for it. You wouldn't spare him any. You killed him."

"Be quiet," Rikimer said. "I'll buy your priesthood. You can bury your friend yourself."

The deacon fell to his knees and beat the rushes with his fists.

Hot wind gusted through the window. There was a long, loud rumble followed by a clap of thunder that nearly lifted Domnola off her feet. Half frightened, she looked out. The sky had darkened and the vultures were gone.

Rikimer went to the door and opened it. "Take care of both of them," he told the steward, jerking his head at the figure on the bed and the one kneeling beside it. He left, without speaking to Domnola. Looking at the dark sky, thinking what she had done for him, Domnola almost cursed him.

XXIX

September 18, 585

THE DEACON MUST BE CALMED. HIS NASTY TONGUE COULD MAKE trouble. Rikimer wasn't afraid of the bishop—he had kept clear, his fees were all rents, always. Legally, he couldn't be touched. But now was no time for a scandal. His mother always believed the worst she heard of him. If she heard her son called a usurer, she would believe it. Back to her knees, and her hair shirt, and her black bread.

He would keep his word on the deacon's promotion. As soon as the drought broke, he would ride to church and tell the priest that he and it were to be part of Valrada's dowry.

His mother would love nothing better than to die a martyr. Let his father die first and she could fast and be damned, but not while her death would pave his father's way to a young bride.

Rikimer kneaded his sweating forehead. The dead Greek's face had reminded him of the boar's; tiny, reddened eyes, foam on its tusks, and then, blood.

A streak of lightning so bright Rikimer saw it through closed lids cleaved the sky; the floor shivered at the thunder. A wind with the smell of old cisterns thrust in through the unglazed window and tumbled the scrolls on Rikimer's desk. From the barns and stables every animal on Poijou began to call, the cattle bellowing their thirst, the horses whinnying. For a moment the din might have been Judgment Day's. Then the rain began.

In the Convent of Ste. Croix, Brunehaut held Ingund

closer than even Ingund could bear for long. "The saddest part," Brunehaut was saying, "is that Claudia never even saw her baby. Antonia sent it to Bordeaux without even letting Claudia kiss it good-bye. I think if I had a baby and no one let me see him, I would go insane."

Valrada considered. "Maybe Antonia's right," she whispered. "Maybe to have your child taken from your arms is what would really destroy you."

September 19, 585

AGAIN TONIGHT LORD RIKIMER HAD RETIRED WITHOUT A WORD to Domnola. There was no way for him to know he owed the drought's breaking to her, and he was angry with her; she dated his mood from Flat-nose's visit.

He would forget Flat-nose's sister when Domnola told him she was with child.

Would he wait to see if the baby was a boy, or would he marry her at once?

What would Antonia do?

Domnola wasn't going to wait to find out.

As she let herself out of the Hall the breeze from the forest bathed Domnola's face with the stench of carrion. At the first orchard she left the road and struck through the trees.

Nothing stirred near Antonia's dark and silent hut.

The roof was easily reached. Domnola's flint struck a

tiny bright seed from her iron and in a moment the thatch bloomed into flame. She fled without looking back.

The door to her room was open. She was sure she'd left it closed. She crept barefoot down the hall. A tall figure stood beside her bed. In Domnola's hand, one sandal knocked against the other and the figure turned.

"Where were you?" said Lord Rikimer.

Domnola let out her breath. "Where would I be, at this hour?" She hadn't expected him to come to her. "Am I supposed to wet my bed?"

"You savage," he said, half-smiling. "There's something under the bed for that."

"Ugh. You *are* a filthy Barbarian. Bretons don't do these things in their bedrooms, make keepsakes of them."

"Come and show me what Bretons do in their bedrooms."

He slept as he walked, silently as a cat. She couldn't sleep. She wished she hadn't consented to ride with him in the morning. Soon after his arrival in August he had lifted her protesting onto a horse and had schooled her relentlessly every day until the terrible drought had put an end to all unnecessary exercise. She had overheard them talking in the kitchen. "Her," the cook Lucia had sneered, "she's never sat on anything but an ass in her life." Their jealousy had steeled Domnola, but she had welcomed the heat that forced him to abandon the project. Tonight, lying there beside her, he had said, "It's time you got back to riding. I have to see the priest, and there's no reason you can't make that trip."

At these words she had lain quite still. He had not ridden to Poijou's church since taking over the villa. What could he want to see its priest about but her? About Flat-nose Lehunsson's sister, he would have gone to Claigne's priest.

She had known he would marry her once the drought broke. Perhaps the ride to the church was a test. Perhaps she had to prove she could ride before she could be a lady. At least the road wouldn't take them past Antonia's. Domnola cursed the faint-heartedness that had hurried her from the scene. Why should she fear hearing one Roman woman scream, she who had seen her whole village—Domnola turned on her side. The way she had left the roof blazing, Antonia would have been suffocated before Domnola was back in the Hall.

If the old hag would have told her what she had done with Lady Big-bottom's son, the fire wouldn't have been necessary.

XXXI

September 20, 585

ONCE OUT OF THE COURTYARD AND ON THE ROAD LORD RIKIMER let his stallion trot. Domnola's gelding would not be left behind. Her saddle began to smack her faster than she could count, relentlessly, jarring her teeth. She began to slip forward and her legs instinctively tightened. At the touch of her knees the gelding was released as if they had sprung a trap. The detestable whapwhapwhapwhap changed to a terrifying wham! wham! wham! each knocking her windless. She had time for one scream between each contact.

She was ready, afterward, to concede that this torture lasted only seconds before Lord Rikimer caught up with her, grabbed her reins, and slowed the gelding to a walk. "These," he held her reins to her, "are reins. Pulling on both reins at once makes the horse stop. Yelling Breton curses and flapping the reins makes the horse go faster. Now take them before I drop them."

"How much further is it?"

"You've been there."

"Why is your church so far from your Hall?"

Lord Rikimer laughed. "Like my grandfather, my uncle Eurik didn't want to live any closer to a Christian church than he had to. My mother's attitude is quite the opposite, as you'll see if you ever visit Antier."

She looked at him sharply, but his face told her that he was only thinking about how his uncle, rather than his father, had taken their father's Hall.

Before he and she returned to that Hall, Antonia's body would have been found, whatever was left of it. No one knew Domnola had left her room but Lord Rikimer himself; of this she was certain. She looked at him more attentively.

There was always work to do in the graveyard. The priest's little mongrel loved this yard work as much as the priest did; in fact their tastes, the priests was finding, were almost perfectly in accord. The dog, which he had named Faustus, had lived with him less than two months and already the priest felt that it must have been sent him expressly by St. Hilary to comfort and support him while he sweated out not just Poijou's drought, but

Poijou's change of masters. He had been instructed by
Lord Dag to read the banns for Lady Valrada's marriage,
but his own future hadn't been referred to.

The priest speared the last leaves on Lady Chrona's
grave and shook the rake over his pile. The dog, who
watched all the priest's actions like a partner on a tricky
and important job, pounced on one impudent stray. The
priest thought of himself momentarily as The Good
Shepherd, with Dog.

Dogs had died in the ditches from Poijou to Poitiers all
August, but this particular dog had dragged its black-
tongued suffering to the priest's door, and the priest, to
his shame, hadn't been able to harden his heart against it.
Christian children were crying for water and he had
succored this soulless creature. Secretly he had let the
dog into the church to lie panting on the cool cement;
moreover when the holy water had grown scummy he
had not poured it out on his dying roses but had held the
dog up to lick the font clean.

All the first week he had never believed the mangy
starveling would live. Now by some miracle it was restored
to extravagant energy, able to follow wherever he went,
barking ferociously at whatever moved on the road beyond
the graveyard gate.

Maybe it was the holy water that had brought about
this miracle. On the other hand, maybe the dog was the
devil, tempting the priest, waiting only until he had been
led so deep into sacrilege there was no denying or
retreating, to disappear in a sulfurous flash.

The priest patted the dog apologetically and turned to
Berto's grave.

There was a sound of approaching hoofbeats and the

dog rushed barking to the graveyard gate. Recognizing the lead rider, the priest murmured two prayers. The dog alternately hurled itself against the gate and scrabbled frantically at its base.

Lord Rikimer drew up in the shade of the church, the girl's horse following. The girl—she was the Breton captive Lady Chrona had bought—was flushed and her hair was disheveled, but what froze the priest's stare and almost made him forget to quiet his dog was her heathen necklace. The dog punctuated the springs by which it now tried in vain to clear the gate, with horrendous barking. The girl's horse stamped nervously; the girl seemed near tears.

"Faustus, sit!" the priest commanded. The dog, quivering, lowered itself. Lord Rikimer dismounted, put his reins through the ring on the priest's tethering post and turned to help the girl. The priest opened the gate.

Hurtling through the gateway the dog clapped its jaws on Lord Rikimer's ankle. The girl's horse bolted before Lord Rikimer could snatch its reins. "Damned cur——." Lord Rikimer sent the dog flying and lunged for his stallion's reins. The girl's horse was galloping northward down the road, mane and tail streaming. After one high yelp the dog came whimpering back to the priest, who stroked it with his foot without taking his eyes from the road, as Lord Rikimer rode off after the runaway.

The girl was crouching low along its neck; her hair flowed out behind her. The priest never had time to pray for her. Something rose up out of the ditch on the road's far side and the runaway horse shied from it in midair. The girl shot forward where the horse's shoulder had been and landed head first, somersaulted once, and crumpled.

The horse galloped on as the vulture in the ditch laboriously lifted its cumbrous dark body in flight and Lord Rikimer reined in beside the girl. The priest began to run.

Same day

THE BABY WAS WIZENED AND CHEESY. BELLA LOOKED BEATIFIC. "Well," Antonia said, "that's that."

Bella's husband all but jumped between her and the door. "Who's going to wash it?"

"Why persecute him?"

The young man stood there, blinking.

"Were you planning on presenting him at court? Listen, that child doesn't need anything the way I need sleep." Antonia had called on Bella at suppertime, decided the child would come that night, and made Bella's man throw her a pelt on the floor. She was too old to get any rest that way. She had been right, though; Bella's labor had begun the hour before dawn.

"What about——"

"Don't stand around; burn all this. Get it out of here." Antonia's head ached for sleep. "Do you want your wife to get a fever?" She turned and pretended to inspect the infant until its father was out of the doorway; then she went home.

The smell warned her.

Antonia stared into what had been her house. The caved-in roof still smoldered.

Everything she had! She grabbed up a dead branch from the edge of the woods and trotted around the ruins poking, fussing like a furious wren. Her cup, her bowl, they were like family at her solitary meals. Her oaken spoon was shaped by her mouth, her fingers, year after year; it fit her, fed her, like a lover. She didn't want a new spoon at her age.

She had counted on her things to make her at home when Lord Rikimer kept his word and sent her to her daughter.

Her unguents. Not a pot left but the few she'd buried.

She'd done well never to take off Claudia's bracelet. It was theft she'd feared, but imagine sifting through all that—she gave the ashes a vicious swipe.

Gratitude to have escaped the fire didn't occur to Antonia. Had she been there, no fire would have been so impudent as to intrude. She knew she hadn't left so much as a spark in the house. It was a mystery, and one with which Antonia had no patience.

She had to wrap her hand to use her trowel; the handle had burned off.

They would give her a pallet at the Hall, but first she would have to tell her story six times. The Hall was a long walk for an old woman who had spent the night on the floor, an old woman who'd worked hard breakfastless, and now this digging.

She would not stress her fatigue to Lord Rikimer. She hadn't abandoned hope that he would keep his promise— naturally she couldn't have been sent anywhere during that drought, but now he would send her. Unless she planted the thought that she was about to croak, that just by stalling he could avoid the expense of paying her off, because she was suddenly "too feeble to stand such a journey."

Grumbling and rehearsing, Antonia stumped down the road.

People stood in murmuring clusters about Poijou's courtyard. They noticed Antonia not at all; or they stared at her, then looked away.

"Eh. Lucia. What's the matter?"

Heads turned as Antonia's ordinary voice rang out. The heads quickly turned away again, as if Antonia had thrown up at table, or her gown had dropped off. Lucia, after one numb glance, stood scraping the pavement with her toe. The steward's grandson filled the gap. "The master's whore——" his excited voice began. Lucia found her tongue.

Antonia stood. A sharp, short pain savaged her heart; she remembered the dark minstrel's enigmatic ballad. . . . *His nurse's hut burned to the ground. . . . And all around was sorrow, But the babe's hair still burned bright.* "Where is the master?" Antonia whispered.

"He's run to his mother's," one of the cooks said spitefully.

"She was afraid of horses, poor thing," another said. "He made her ride."

"I wouldn't have his dreams now for nuthin'."

"Him! He don't dream. He. . . ."

Antonia backed away. The women went on muttering, absorbed. Antonia edged between them. Out of the courtyard, she tried to walk faster. She watched her feet,

one following the other; her sandal straps kept blurring.
Once on the high road at last, she turned her haggard
face north.

XXXIII

September 26, 585

STEAMING BESIDE THE CONVENT'S HOT WATER TANK, VALRADA
generally found her eyes fleeing upward to the windows
which more than oversupplied the room with light. The
way the bathers' wet shifts stuck to them, they might as
well have been naked; conducted to the baths their first
day at Ste. Croix, Valrada and Brunehaut had thought
they would die. In the month that had since lapsed they
had learned to cope—Brunehaut by keeping her attention
rigidly on Ingund, Valrada somewhat less successfully by
studying the framed sky. Valrada could also have studied
Ingund, but seeing her do so always gave Brunehaut a
smug look that made Valrada want to pinch her. She was
wearing that look right now. Ingund had learned to turn
over lately; in the middle of the towel Brunehaut had
spread for her, the dripping child was rolling from back to
stomach to back to stomach like a pony in the dust.
Brunehaut, catching Valrada admiring, as Brunehaut
supposed, this phenomenal performance, smiled; Valrada
slid her eyes to the wall beyond.

Brunehaut stood up. "We're going on."

Valrada raised one eyebrow. Brunehaut expected her to
leap up and follow. Brunehaut thought it an incom-

parable treat for Valrada to sit in the unguentarium and watch Ingund get oiled.

In her father's house at Clermont, Sister Portia had told Valrada, the bath rooms' stucco had been painted with scenes at whose details Sister Portia would only hint. For a spinster nun, Sister Portia was remarkably informed, and though her conversation was more suggestive than expository, Valrada had learned more than one thing from her. From Brunehaut, due to the constraint that the particular circumstances of her marriage placed between them, Valrada had learned nothing. Lord Eurik was one person neither ever mentioned to the other.

Valrada had heard, from someone who'd seen him do it on a wager, that Alarik could ride Storm under an arch, grasp the ring of its keystone, and with the strength of his thighs alone, prevent the horse from moving forward. She, if God and her uncle granted, would feel...the imagined Alarik became so palpable that her scalp prickled. If he really were present—if she should look up and find him seeing her virtually naked like this....

"Someone insists on seeing you, Valrada," Sister Justina said disapprovingly from only three yards away. Valrada nearly strangled.

The guest who had bulled her way through Ste. Croix's formalities had followed Sister Justina into the room. Not Alarik. Antonia.

The old midwife looked like Mary Magdalene in the desert. Sister Justina left with her neck stretched straight up like a peacock's; Valrada could imagine how Antonia must have talked to her. "How did *you* get here?"

"We must speak privately, *mea Domina*."

"There's no such thing as privacy in this place!" The

two or three nuns who had been bathing were staring at Antonia, who clutched her tunic as if they were foreign soldiery bent on getting a look at her navel. A bench stood near the spot where the continuous noise of water sobbing into the tank would cover their words, and Valrada led this shockingly caved-in edition of Antonia over to it. She could guess what had happened. The midwife had given Rikimer some of her impudence and Rikimer had set her on the road.

Antonia's impatience to report seemed suddenly to collapse. She sagged on her bench like a burst pig bladder, her jaws jammed together as if she suspected Valrada of coveting her teeth. Valrada glared at the three nuns and they retreated to the far end of the tank. "The drought," Valrada prodded. "Has it broken on Poijou?"

"Lady Brunehaut has a son."

Might God do to Rikimer whatever he had done to this poor old crone to smash her wits.

"The girl I gave her is Claudia's."

"Antonia?"

"Lord Rikimer made me. He threatened us all— Nicolaus and the Breton and me. He threatened to kill us if Lady Brunehaut had a son. He made us swear we would smother it before it suckled. But I didn't, *mea Domina*. The boy is alive, I swear!"

"*Antonia?*"

First the Breton had come to Antonia's hut and gone, looking, so she said, for Lady Valrada. Then Rikimer himself had ridden up. He hadn't bothered to dismount. He'd kept her standing in the June sun while he remarked on her hut's solitude. A vulnerable spot, he'd observed. Her heart had quickened; it had suspected what was coming, if she had not.

Then he had looked right at her and told her what he expected her to do.

He could find damnation, she had answered, without her help.

He had gone on coolly inspecting the forest where it edged almost into her yard. He'd heard she did things in that forest that could get her burned, he confided.

"You don't have to do anything," he said. "Just refrain. Let it strangle on its own guck."

Greek Nicolaus had waited for her to come to him. He was suddenly wearing a new gold fillet, but he agreed that for no price and no threat could Lord Rikimer make him kill an unbaptized child. The Breton, Nicolaus had suggested, was too ignorant of Christianity to have this scruple. Ten days later Claudia had given birth to a girl and Antonia had told Nicolaus to leave everything to her.

Antonia caught hold of Valrada's shift. "I begged Lady Brunehaut to have her baby in Poitiers, *mea Domina!*"

"What did you do with Lady Brunehaut's child?"

Antonia let go. "I gave him to a wet nurse," she whispered.

"My *God*, is he on Poijou?"

Antonia slid off the bench to her knees. "I sent him where Lord Rikimer could never find him, *mea Domina*. I saved his life, *mea Domina*." Valrada's hands gripped the old woman's shoulders. Antonia's cheek muscles seemed to snap. "I gave him to...the woman...the woman who brought back your brother's falcon."

There was a great splash as Antonia's back hit the hot water. She flailed frantically in the tank at Valrada's feet. "You didn't!" Valrada screamed. "You witch! You didn't!"

A nun got to Antonia before the old woman could drown. The prioress and her attendants ran in through one door, women from the oiling room through the other.

Valrada whirled to Brunehaut. In Brunehaut's arms, Ingund clung like a monkey. "Brunehaut!" Valrada's arm pointed at the wretched choking figure at tank's edge. "Brune-haut!" Sister Justina, misjudging Valrada's rising arm, grabbed it. "*Will* you get away, you stupid Roman?" Valrada flung her off.

Brunehaut thrust her shoulder between Valrada and Sister Justina's slap. "My sister and I need to talk undisturbed," she suggested coolly.

Sister Justina had dealt with Franks right off the land before and learned the wisdom of letting them work off some of their savagery on each other. Valrada was already going for her clothes. The old slave seemed uninjured. "The herb garden," Sister Justina told Brunehaut stiffly. "Sister Portia will wait just outside the door and she will call me the *instant* there is any——"

"Yes, yes," said Brunehaut; she hurried to dress.

XXXIV

Same day

SISTER PORTIA TOOK HER POST IN THE HALL BY THE GARDEN DOOR; Valrada arrived first. "Don't talk to me!" she urged, and swept by, face averted. A second after the door closed on Valrada, Sister Portia was aghast to see the old slave Valrada had attacked coming down the hall. One of the youngest novices was supporting her arm. Brunehaut was nowhere in sight.

"Lady Valrada asked to be alone," Sister Portia lied. The old woman—she had been given a novice's gown but her hair wasn't even dry yet—surely shouldn't go into the garden with Valrada alone.

"She'll see me." Antonia raised her voice as Sister Portia continued to block the door. "She'll see me, Sister."

The door flew open and Valrada snatched the old slave by the upper arms, almost lifting her over the sill. Sister Portia had shrunk back as the door opened; now she pulled it halfway closed behind the pair in the garden and leaned toward it. "Now sit down and talk fast! You could lose your——" she heard Valrada say, before the little novice reached around her and self-righteously shut the door.

When Domnola had come to fetch Antonia to Lady Brunehaut's delivery, Antonia had laid Claudia's daughter, drugged, in her long basket and covered her with cloths. Had Lady Brunehaut's baby been a girl, Claudia's would have been returned to Antonia's hut without ever being uncovered. As it was, the new heir to Poijou had been fed the same semi-poison and taken from Brunehaut's room before Valrada's very eyes, under the rags that earlier had concealed the older baby.

At the dark of the moon he had been drugged again and given to the forest woman.

"Oh *God*, how *could* you?"

"It was to save his life, *mea Domina*."

For a piece of the gold bracelet Claudia had paid her, a hide merchant had ignored Antonia's lack of a travel permit and had let her ride all the way to Poitiers on one of his carts. All during the journey Antonia had done nothing but think about what she would say.

Valrada listened, white as a corpse. "The Breton must have told your cousin the boy was alive somewhere, *mea Domina*. She thought your cousin meant to marry her. He must have decided it was easier to kill her and Greek Nicolaus and me than to find the child and kill him."

"Marry her. And how much did he bribe *you?*"

"Nothing, *mea Domina*."

"Nonsense!"

"St. Hilary slay me if I lie, your ladyship's cousin never gave me anything!"

"What did he *promise* to give you?"

"Nothing, *mea Domina*."

Valrada shot to her feet: "You greedy liar, if you think I——"

"Freedom, *mea Domina*," Antonia whispered.

"Freedom! Sweet *Mary*, what more could you have had if you'd been free? Were you whipped, were you stabled with other animals as filthy as yourself? Were——"

Valrada stopped abruptly as Brunehaut, Ingund in her arms, stepped into the garden.

Brunehaut seated herself facing Antonia. "Now listen," Valrada said: "Antonia is *not* crazy, so don't waste time wondering." Unable to listen or watch, she turned quickly away.

Long steps had taken Valrada almost to the garden's far corner before Brunehaut's screams brought her running back. "Don't waste time!" she cut through Brunehaut's stammer. "We've got to find your son before Rikimer does. Send for Claudia."

Brunehaut leaped up. "No!" Backing off, she clutched Ingund so tightly the child began to cry.

Brunehaut's eyes glittered like a cornered animal's. Valrada stood quite still and spoke gently. "She will have to be told."

"No!" Brunehaut sobbed.

"You can keep *both*. You can keep *both* babies, Brunehaut. Claudia gave her child to *your slave:* Ingund belongs to you. But you *must* have Claudia's testimony to claim your son. You see that. I'll send Sister Portia for Claudia." Whatever the law was, Valrada was certain the bishop wasn't going to take Ingund away from the Lady of Poijou and give her to an unmarried freed girl.

Claudia's eyes were wary. Sister Portia, Valrada guessed, had told her about the arrival of Poijou's midwife, and about that swim. Claudia stationed herself nearer to Brunehaut than Valrada and tried to read both their faces at once; Antonia hadn't raised hers.

"Claudia, no one is angry with you," Valrada said. Claudia waited. "You had a daughter, Midsummer's Eve?"

Claudia glanced once at Antonia. "Yes, *mea Domina.*" The Roman girl seemed to begin a study of her sandals.

"You gave Antonia your lover's gold bracelet to send the child to her daughter in Bordeaux?"

Claudia's voice stayed toneless; the "Yes, *mea Domina*" was a little slower coming.

"Antonia lied to you, and she wants to return what remains of your bracelet."

Startled, Antonia took a moment to react. Valrada waited implacably. Claudia's wary look had changed to alarm. She made no move to take the broken circlet out of Antonia's hand. "The child is alive," said Valrada. Mechanically, her eyes fixed on Valrada's, Claudia accepted the forfeited gold. Valrada took a deep breath.

"Claudia, your child is here." Claudia stared at her as if Valrada had forgotten to speak Latin. "This is your daughter," Valrada said gently.

Claudia's hands dropped the half-bracelet; her uncomprehending gaze wavered to Antonia. The midwife's somber eyes looked through her. As if it weighed a thousand pounds, Claudia dragged her focus to Brunehaut's face. Brunehaut stood as she had stood since Claudia's entry into the garden, resolutely still. Claudia looked at Ingund. Her eyes filled. Glancing once at Valrada, who nodded—just—she tentatively reached out and touched Ingund's foot.

With a sudden hiss Brunehaut slapped Claudia and burst into tears.

Valrada was beside Claudia with one step. One hand pressed the bracelet back into Claudia's hand; the other she laid for a moment on Claudia's back. At this touch Claudia also burst into tears. "Wait outside," Valrada murmured, then rounded on Antonia: "You go with her, hell singe you! And try not to let the devil take you till you've helped straighten out the mess you've made!"

Brunehaut crumpled onto her bench, rocking and sobbing. Frightened, Ingund whimpered and struggled in her clutch. Valrada bent and laid her arm across Brunehaut's shaking shoulders. "Alarik will find your baby."

The back under her arm seemed to deflate; it shuddered and was still. Brunehaut raised her ravaged face. In the new silence she seemed to become aware for the first time of Ingund's cries: Automatically she gave Ingund her breast, but for a second a grim expression passed over her face. This was followed by a look so tender Valrada's heart was wrung. Then Brunehaut lifted her eyes again and Valrada saw nothing in them but horror. "Two months!" Brunehaut whispered. "Two months, unbaptized, with...with those...*those in the forest!* We must go to Sister Radegonda *at once!*"

"We'll sound like a couple of country Franks gone mad behind walls. They'll slap a guard on us faster than Mother Agnes can think of a nice name for it. And talk? What one eavesdropper overhears, everybody in the convent knows before matins, and what one sister knows, Rikimer's priest can find out in one visit to the chaplain's house." Valrada sat down. "Nobody's going to listen to us till we have the child to show."

"They'll never give him to us! They'll swear Antonia's lying! They'll give us some other child, and swear it's mine! He'll never be rescued, and she *didn't baptize him!*" Ingund had let the nipple slip from her lips and her face was coloring to roar; Brunehaut seemed barely aware that she held a child. Valrada gripped Brunehaut's shoulders and the rising voice dropped: "Get Sister Radegonda. Get her."

"She *won't help us*, Brunehaut. She *won't*. She's old, and sonless; what can she do? Why should she help if she could? Franks killed her whole family."

"Mother Agnes, then."

"*She'd* tell us to put it all in writing."

Brunehaut, though she had acted unconscious of the Roman's scorn for their illiteracy, now took Valrada's point, Valrada noted, quickly enough. "Sister Justina," Brunehaut said. "Her orders carry as much weight as Mother Agnes's."

"That woman laid hands on me."

"She's been prioress for years. She forgot herself."

Valrada felt her temper fly up like a bent branch

loosed. "If you actually propose to go for help to a woman who *handled* me like a *slave*, you'll go without me! Brunehaut, who is going to believe what we say because we say it: Alarik, or a Roman? Who knows the forest: Alarik, or a nun? Who will go any distance, any——"

"How will you send for him?"

Valrada exhaled. "I think," her eyes glinted, "that's something Claudia can arrange."

There was a great wet spot in the lap of Claudia's gown where, Valrada guessed, she must have been burying her face. Valrada tried to resummon her austerely, and Antonia, calmly. If Claudia were too much sympathized with before Brunehaut could arrange a marriage for her a good way from Poijou, she might hold out for some more troublesome arrangement. As for Antonia, she mustn't be throttled until Rikimer had lost.

Claudia approached reluctantly, her eyes studiously avoiding Ingund.

"Do you still take flowers every Sunday to my father's grave?"

"Oh, yes, *mea Domina*."

"Have you met a young man on these trips?"

Claudia's hopeful looked vanished. "No, *mea Domina!*"

"No one, never?"

"I swear to God, *mea Domina*."

"Ah. We need someone to carry a message to Antier."

Claudia put her hand to her mouth. Valrada twisted Alarik's signet ring and waited. "I could...I probably *could* meet someone——"

"Please do."

"We don't have time for that," Brunehaut protested. "We need someone right *now*, we have to be *sure*, we——"

"She is sure," said Valrada. "Aren't you, Claudia?"
Claudia didn't look at her. "Yes, *mea Domina.*"

"Well, then." Valrada spread her handkerchief beside
her on the bench, took off her ring, pricked her finger,
and bloodied her leaping deer. "I ought to use *your* blood,"
she told Antonia between her teeth, "if I thought you had
any, you heartless demon." She stamped her
handkerchief. The ring had been cut for sealing wax, but
the deer's dyed outline, at least, was plain—plain enough
for Alarik Alansson.

XXXV

October 4, 585

ALARIK MADE THEM ALL REPEAT THEIR STORIES OVER AND OVER,
listening for what grew, what was forgotten. He
questioned them like a duke holding court. Valrada, he
could see, would have strangled him had he not been her
only hope. Such a story, however, had to be examined.
Women were excitable. Valrada jumped to conclusions as
rashly as a squirrel. The old midwife might be senile. The
Roman girl looked like the kind who says what she judges
her mistress wants to hear. Even Brunehaut, since
becoming a mother, seemed as volatile and unreasonable
as all the other women Alarik had ever known.

So Rikimer was everything Valrada had said and more.
With a less hopeful heart than he let them see, Alarik
promised to be their champion. This vow by no means

satisfied Brunehaut: She wanted him to promise success. There was no use talking to women when they got the wind up, and Alarik didn't try. Valrada, however, turned on poor Brunehaut some of the flaming anger he knew he himself had lit with his inquisition, and Brunehaut subsided, miserable. The greatest kindness he could do her was to go quickly; he paused only to give Valrada the necklace he had meant to be her wedding gift. If he never returned from the forest, she should have it.

She had him put it on her, just as he'd imagined doing. As he lowered his hands to her shoulders, she looked straight into his eyes. His throat grew hard, and for a moment his hands gripped her shoulders, but then he remembered where he was and how many eyes were turned on them, and the rest was not as he had imagined. He stepped back, even as he saw that this devastated her. He turned, trying to keep his breathing inaudible, and without looking again at any of them, he left her.

He rode straight for the monastery of St. Leonard's.

The last ten miles ran through the forest's outskirts. At the monastery, the road ended.

He told the monks he was going hunting. As he had neither spear nor bow and showed no sign of madness— beyond an inflexible determination to enter the forest which they dreaded—they were skeptical. Their warnings were first deft hints, then blunt.

Alarik believed at least half what they said. He asked for their prayers.

Squeezing, twisting, sometimes crawling, with Storm obediently forcing a way after him, he made his way through thickets so dense neither he nor the patient horse could take two steps until he cut their way. There was one comfort. It would be hard for anyone to steal up on him.

People said that mutilated outlaws could find refuge with the First Ones. Alarik could half believe it. A man with a branded cheek or missing nose would have little to hope for on the outside however many years passed; the Wise People might think they could trust him never to desert and betray them. Some whispered they insured this—that a man had to be willing to be hamstrung for his bread and roof. He would be kept for breeding like a wing-clipped cob, but at least he would see his sons grow up hunters. Others said he would be blinded as well as lamed.

Panting, Alarik leaned back against a vine-imprisoned dogwood to rest. The dogwood was hung with berries; he took his throwing hatchet from his belt and freed the lowest branch so he could pull it down within plundering reach.

The hatchet—*Skull-smasher*—had been his father's.

In late afternoon the copse began to thin a little. A more fanciful man might have found something deliberate about the wall he was tunneling through. A giant could have observed that it ran along the forest's perimeter almost neatly. To this whimsy, however, Alarik would have pointed out that the trees were getting taller as he fought his way, their shade thicker, and so the vines and undergrowth which threatened to choke the trees at the forest's edge might themselves predictably be suffocated at its heart.

Once, as he rested, a rabbit gradually manifested itself a trifling throw away, but though his grip on Skull-smasher tightened he didn't allow his arm to so much as twitch. Watching the rabbit's delicately surveying ears he felt his own pulled back, his neck muscles tensing to kill, but he controlled every other muscle, and the rabbit nibbled its fill. It would be trying the saints to send up smoke and then pray for protection from cutthroats. He supped on bread and cheese.

Storm's tail had accumulated as much detritus as a storm-littered shoreline. One at a time, Alarik liberated enough burrs to fill a shoe.

She'd worn deerhide shoes that day he'd held her horse. He'd thought the stubble must hurt her through such thin soles, but she had never flinched. Realizing that her brother and cousin found her presence worse than extraneous, she would not have admitted it if her feet had bled. He had liked her pluck.

Rikimer's stud had burst from rest almost to full speed; Alarik had never regretted his lost stallion more. "Rikimer's horse is stupid," she'd said. Since then, he and she had often baffled one another, but in that first fatal interview they had read each other's thoughts like twins.

There was no need to hobble Storm in this tangle. Alarik knelt beside his saddlebags and got out his cloak, and one other thing.

Antonia the midwife had followed him out of Ste. Croix's garden. "Take this." She'd put a tiny clay pot into his hand. Two nuns appeared in the corridor, and Antonia paused until they were gone. Then she came a step closer. "Lady Brunehaut's son hasn't been christened," she murmured. "There will be many days between finding him, and Christian country." Brunehaut had said something like that, and had given Alarik a crucifix on a silver chain to fasten around the child's neck the moment he had the child in his hands. "Rub this," Antonia peered up at Alarik with peculiar intensity, "just in the center of the baby's forehead. It will ward off the Evil Eye." She stared at Alarik until the beginning of something in his eyes apparently satisfied her. "Do it at once. Keep his hands off it, and when that first skin peels, do it again. "That should be enough. You can tell." She emphasized the last words, her eyes fixed on Alarik's unblinking as a falcon's. Alarik had turned and left without a word. The ointment, however, he had packed with Brunehaut's crucifix.

Now he stood up, lowered his breeches to expose the white skin of his inner thighs, and daubed a spot.

Stretching out on the saddlepad, he arranged his two bags carefully beside him. In his sleep they might give him the illusion that someone lay there, and so help him to the dream he tried every night to recapture.

The stags were in rut and as the moon rose he could hear them bellowing to the does, sick of love, and not to be comforted with a few windfalls.

There was no use wondering which, when he and Rikimer locked horns, would be the better man. He shut his eyes and began painstakingly to remember the dream he had been given at Poitiers, the night before the arrow had taken Lord Eurik between the eyes.

He had tried countless times, recalling the dream feature by feature, but though this always had certain immediate effects, he had never successfully resummoned the dream.

He was wakened by broad daylight and a scream.

He jerked upright to see a great golden eagle plummet out of the sky, to land like a thunderbolt on a gigantic snake.

The eagle's powerful wings beat the air but couldn't lift

its prize. Suddenly out of the brush a vixen rushed the eagle with all the ferocity of a mother defending her cub. One slash from the vixen's needle teeth was enough to make the eagle release the snake; one blow from its wings knocked the vixen to the ground. Beak and talons were into her flesh on the instant.

The thought of interfering didn't enter Alarik's mind: Between the hunger of two wild creatures, there was no difference in virtue. Then the writhing vixen's face turned his way and he saw for the first time that it was scarred; a vertical white streak ran from eye to curled-back lip. He snatched Skull-smasher from its sheath and hurled it at the eagle.

He awoke to darkness. He heard his drowsy gelding shift its feet. Skull-smasher lay in its sheath where he had placed it when he unbuckled his belt.

He had not dreamed of that vixen since Toulouse.

The place on his thigh where he'd daubed Antonia's salve was hot. Determinedly he shut his eyes.

Pale sunlight chivvied them open. Storm stood nearby. The spot on Alarik's thigh was sore. He took a look at it.

He had held Lord Eurik's forehead between his hands, and without closing his eyes he could see again the not quite circular mark with the Poitevin shaft protruding not an inch below it, as if the archer had aimed at a bull's-eye and just missed. The red spot on his own leg was a fair approximation of this bull's eye. The color was angrier, but might fade with the soreness.

He didn't know what he was going to do.

XXXVI

October 8, 585

THE POOL WAS THE FIRST WATER ALARIK HAD FOUND SINCE THE monks', but he felt a strange absence of elation. A breeze that shimmered with milkweed silk rustled through the reeds and set their plumes waving . . . yet the impression the pool gave was of stillness.

No wailing chorus of gnats assailed his ears, no cautious frog broke surface at his approach; the reflected swaying of the reeds was the pool's only life. The smooth surface was unmarred by scum, a seductive mirror. The unease at the pit of Alarik's stomach changed to decision and instead of leading his excited horse toward the reed bed he began to drag the baffled animal back up the slope, away from what Alarik could not doubt was poisoned water.

Halfway up the long slope he heard a water bird.

Stories of the fatal will-o'-the-wisp came to mind as the short high notes exploded again, clearer than before. He thrust one finger between neck and tunic and by its chain, fished out his crucifix. Holding the cross between thumb and two fingers, he led Storm toward his new hope.

An anxious hum became the backdrop for the dipper's calls. The brush became thicker and Alarik tucked his cross between his lips so as to free one hand. Pushing through willows he came to where the earth had been cut raggedly away. Between two low banks hairy with uncovered roots, flowed the weak descendant of the floods which had roared this channel clear.

Midstream, the dipper teetered on a rock. Just as Alarik saw the bird it dived; when it reappeared a back swimmer kick in its beak. Alarik released his horse.

A narrow beach of soft sandy earth was liberally pasted with exhausted willow leaves, but as Alarik knelt to refill his wineskin his eye was caught by deer tracks. He turned his face resolutely away.

By late afternoon he was riding again, slowly. Just before dusk he came upon an ivy-shrouded tree rising out of a bowllike depression. The vines traveling from the bowl's lip to the tree's branch tips were so closely spaced that the hollow under the tree was as curtained off as a lady's *rheda*. Only moss grew in that shade, thick and soft. The ivy was in bloom, and bees gave the tree a lulling hum.

Had it been his wedding night he couldn't have wished a better bedchamber. He felt his throat grow tight and passed his hand over it; his chin was bristly as boar's hide, and the thought of himself as bridegroom in that condition somewhat diminished the tree's spell.

He had checked the spot on his thigh at midday and found that it had formed a thin blister; now he saw that this gray film of skin had been broken and was wrinkling back from the redness underneath. The soreness, however, was gone.

In the middle of the night he woke with the feeling of being observed so strong the hair stood on his head.

He was surrounded by eyes that glowed at him out of the dark. His heart jumped like a thief, but even before it had dropped back into place his mind had lurched enough further from sleep to let him see that these eyes were too tiny for his fears. Hundreds of silent avid moths were working the moonlit ivy.

She was not ready to deal with him yet.

The spot he had painted on his leg had itched all night, but it was dry, the raised cuticle detached and lost somewhere in his breeches-leg. He unpacked Antonia's little pot again and carefully redaubed the spot.

He rode north as before.

There was a melange of tracks at the stream where he watered Storm, but none that quickened his heart, neither of the deer that he might not hunt nor the other quarry that he must. He didn't expect to find the Old Ones so few days' journey from plowed land, though for a moment last night he'd thought they had found him.

He made camp that night beside a red-leafed oak sapling so wound about by vines that it would not, he judged, survive another season. He set Skull-smasher to freeing it.

The dangling stems gave the oak the look of a ship with all sheets in the wind, but there was a dignity in the resistance it had made that reminded Alarik that once its race had been sacred to his own—before King Clovis had brought the Franks to Gaul.

A flock of starlings were performing their evening drill above the biggest tree—an oak, probably the sapling's parent. The starlings maneuvered in perfect unison, rising and sinking, wheeling and turning as one bird as they sang their evening hymn. When they settled, they filled the great tree.

Their ritual complete, they were their jaunty, garrulous selves again, like soldiers after field mass. Alarik welcomed them. Whatever an intruder's stealth, the high-posted sentinels would rouse their whole flock to cacophony in good time.

In the morning the starlings' oak was a gray hill. Storm, peacefully browsing several yards away, could have been a sailing barge becalmed. The mist hid the landmarks Alarik had chosen the night before, but he rode what he was reasonably sure was north.

When the mist lifted, he found that the great parent oak he had slept near was a juvenile compared to those he now found himself under. Any one of their trunks could have stabled three horses. The air was heavy with the smell of thousands of years of moldering oak leaves. There was no other kind of tree in sight.

He sat gazing about. He had never been in a pure oak forest before, and yet he felt he was returning as much as discovering. His own great-grandfather had paid homage to the gods of these trees, before the god of Clovis's Roman wife had promised the Franks Gaul in exchange for exclusive fealty. This bargain had suited King Clovis; Alarik didn't know what choice his own grandsire would have made, given a choice.

The discovery of the oaks' domain at once numbed and exhilarated him. He realized that all his life he had yearned to journey deep into the forest, to be as lost to the world of pastures and spires as the sponge-diver is lost to the world of air and dust—to lose in this awful twilight all that discontented him with himself, as the naked diver's soil and sweat are washed away in the blue Aegean; to lose at last all his human needs—as the diver ceases to breathe when he sinks into the sea.

But when he closed his eyes he saw Valrada, and only Valrada, and he resigned himself to the knowledge that as no forest was so deep he would not penetrate it for her, so no plain was so treeless but that he would follow her there.

In the morning the mark on his leg was red-brown like

an old burn. Staring at it he came to a decision about Antonia. "The spell is broken," she had said, "if the spellmaker speaks of it. Ever, to anyone. Wife, priest, brother, *the child himself.* If the spell is ever explained it becomes not a protection but a curse." Alarik had turned and left while she was gabbling. He would persuade Brunehaut, he decided now, to send Antonia to her daughter in Bordeaux. Brunehaut could call it punishment or Christian forgiveness, as her mood indicated, but leave Poijou Antonia must.

XXXVII

October 13, 585

FOUR DAYS AFTER HE HAD FREED THE VINE-CHOKED OAKLING, Alarik rode across a clearing and found himself in a stand of young beeches. His hair, though he realized at once that he should have been expecting them, rose on his nape.

As he anticipated, the slender beeches were the first tone of a swelling chord, and he was soon riding among gray titans as ancient and majestic as the oaks whose domain had so abruptly ended. He rode steadfastly north, seeing nothing but beech trees.

He killed the first rabbit he surprised and ate the liver, raw and steaming, on the spot. He tied the gutted rabbit to his saddle by its ears and rode on. It was in this ash-gray zone that he expected to find or be found by those he sought.

Which and when, they would decide.

As he began to make evening camp he heard rustling overhead, and the grind of tooth on hull—a squirrel surely. As if to answer this thought, his upturned face was pattered with nibbled husk. Searching for the creature, his startled eyes discovered mistletoe berries glinting among the beech leaves; he crossed himself and left.

It wasn't long before it occurred to him that a squirrel should have scolded his intrusion vehemently. For a second he thought the rabbit liver was coming back up. The small of his back felt watched. He had never believed those stories about cut Achilles tendons and burned eyes, but his own eyes prickled and he found himself reaching down to rub the back of his ankles.

He slept badly, hearing all night the rush of wings flying south—as if every breathing thing was fleeing counter to his own course. The morning sky, where he could glimpse it, was a moving mass of southward-flying ducks; he fought down the feeling that unchecked could grow to panic, the sense of traveling into something from which those more knowing fled. He felt as a man forcing his way through terror-stricken refugees into a burning city would feel.

He flushed no game all day.

Just at sunset he came upon a bed of cream-colored mushrooms. Their shape was unfamiliar, but their tops were so lacy from nibbling slugs that he picked with confidence.

He crumbled the slender-stalked fungi into enough simmering water to fill him, wondering, as he first knocked the slugs off, how much hungrier he would have to be to leave the slimy creatures on.

The soup tasted rancid. He set it down and rechecked

Storm's tethering. He shook out his saddle bags and repacked them. He banked his fire for the night. The moon was showing before he sat down with his back against a beech trunk, held his breath, and drank.

Five minutes later he was leaning back against his tree, breathing hard. The nausea passed, but the mushrooms' bitterness continued to blow back up his throat. To distract himself he decided to check Storm's tether one more time, but when he stood up he discovered he was too unsteady. He staggered to his sheepskin and lay down.

With his head in his saddle the dizziness went away. In fact, he thought he had never felt so well.

Certainly he had never felt so awake.

As he gazed at the beeches their random placement took on order and he saw they were the pillars of an immense cathedral. That nearest where he lay was luminous gray stone, the next was white polished marble spiraled with sapphires, as if a blue ribbon had been wound around a swan's breast. Every sapphire seemed to contain a star; Alarik's eyes followed their winding course up the moonlit column to the cathedral's open dome, and as he began again to look at the moon, it welled larger and larger until it filled the sky.

The moon's light bathed and cooled him so that he felt cleaner than he had ever felt, as if he had been given back his first skin. This moonlight coolness was delicious; he had never felt precisely that perfection of temperature on every inch of his body.

He looked straight at the moon's center and at once its brightness intensified. This concentrated brightness grew out from the moon's center like a drop of dye spreading in a bowl of milk, until at last the whole of his vision was light. He felt at once exalted and on the brink of still greater exaltation. It occurred to him that he had died and was about to see God, that the form which was gradually swirling into being in the center of the great field of light would be God, but as he stared he saw that the shape was a woman's. She was at once made of the light and the source of the light. He felt terror and supreme happiness, which he could not separate. She opened her arms to him and he saw that she was Valrada and his soul left his body and rose up to her.

Storm was gone. Alarik calmed his first panic; the horse was too healthy to go far without leaving unmistakable traces; Alarik resolved to walk around his campsite in growing concentric circles until he found the first pile. How Storm had come untied was a mystery. He himself was so devastated by the loss of what he had dreamed that the really serious loss of his horse seemed no great thing.

The ashes of his supper fire were cold. He felt a second flood of dismay as he realized that he had no feeling for how long he'd slept; it might have been days. He started to reassure himself from his night's growth of stubble that it had not, remembered—too late to stop his rising hand—that he hadn't shaved in more than a week, and rubbed his hand across his jaw. His heart hit his throat. His chin was as smooth as his forehead.

Panting, he clapped his suddenly clammy palm to his chest: His crucifix hung there still. The saddlebags still lay beside his sheepskin. He tore them open.

Nothing was missing.

He forced his breathing steady. There no use looking for Storm. He buckled on Skull-smasher and his sword. His saddle, his blanket and his packs he would just have to lug. He started north. Every time leaves rustled he stiffened. He thought of all he had ever been told of poisoned arrows, and his fresh-shaved skin seemed to burn.

After about half an hour the beechwood sloped down to a lake. The shore was marshy, all mud and bogholes. He thought of the mare he had watched sink under just such reeds in Brittany, and set down his load. Whether he proceeded along the lake's eastern or western shore was surely important. He found a beechnut and tossed it as far across the reeds toward open water as he could. He stood and watched where his offering sank, letting his field of vision expand from there.

To his right, the forest's slope was steepest; in the shallows to his left a heron was fishing.

The heron's back was the color of the beech trunks, its sticklike legs two more reeds in the multitude; he had looked at the bird a minute before seeing it.

The thin water would be iced over in a week and the heron gone. Possibly it would rest and feed at the Bourre on its way to the warm sea. God knew if *he* would ever see Poijou again.

A flock of ducks circled, swooping low to investigate the shining water, then, dissatisfied, wary over something—perhaps himself, perhaps, his skin prickled, someone else—they poured upward again and on. He heard a bittern's rapid clucks and turned his head; the bird was somewhere among the weeds by the shore. Searching them for it he noticed almost a sort of path through the sedge tufts, as if a boat had been rowed over them. His gut went lead-heavy. The sudden splash of the heron's bill made him jump as if someone had shrieked.

The heron's neck reared back out of the water, a snake writhing on its beak. With the speed of a coiled spring the heron tossed the water snake and caught it square in the gullet. The bird glared impersonally around, then with arrogant deliberation rose out of the water and flew with stately measured wingbeats, oblivious of the man who watched it pass in front of him and light not thirty feet away. The spider claws closed over a twisted beech branch that overhung the bank at its steepest point. The bird gave one or two rasping croaks and hunched into truculent silence. Its shadow was a strange shape on the bank beside the broad band cast by the tree's trunk.

The snake the heron had swallowed live seemed to be wrapping its cold coils around Alarik's own bowels. He was not, it had dawned on him, looking at the shadow of the trunk; what he was seeing fell at the wrong angle to the shadow of the heron. He had been looking at a path. This path led *into* the hill.

He picked up his saddle, his pad, and his bags. The heron flew off on his approach, and this time he didn't watch to see where it would land. He walked down the ramplike excavation into the chambered hall and found the old woman waiting for him.

He was in a dimly lit anteroom. Whatever was beyond was dark and curtained off. He wondered what was there, and whether he would be brought to it or it to him. He wondered how many were there, and whether the heavy stone door he had found open would be swung shut behind him.

The ceiling was too low for him, but he balked at his first impulse—to drop to one knee. The old woman was seated like a queen; he would not appear to kneel to her.

He laid down his load and squatted. In the lamplight, the old woman's eyes seemed to glint.

"I bring you a friendship token from the lady of Poijou," he said.

"You bring more than that, I think. The lady of Poijou could not expect my small people to carry so much."

"No...lady...would expect *me* to carry so much. I lost my horse—not far from here."

"A horse is wasted on a man who could lose it."

He shut his teeth.

His eyes were accustoming themselves to the scant light and he decided that he must be in a storeroom. The corner behind the old woman's elbow was taken up with large closed jars—the biggest the height of his breastbone, the next beside it a hand shorter, several others, smaller. The room smelled of earth and disuse and some kind of perfume—in the lamp oil, he supposed—and something unpleasant. He extracted a silk-wrapped bracelet from his pack and the old woman—Valrada said her name was Liguria, but he wouldn't count on it—took it from his hand, but didn't look at it. "The lady of Poijou has never greeted me before."

"She greets you now."

Liguria unfolded the silk. The bracelet, made of two silver-mounted boar tusks, was a part of his share from Convenae which he had suspected neither Brunehaut nor Valrada would care to own. Liguria put it in the bag that hung from her waist. "The hand that gives, gathers. What do you seek?"

"I have come for the boy you took from Poijou three moons back."

Liguria coughed, and the curtains behind her parted. A young woman came silently into the chamber bearing a woven stool which at her mistress's nod she set in front of Alarik, then retreated behind the curtain without ever having looked at him. "I did not steal the boy. I paid for him."

Alarik nodded and sat down on the woven stool. "I am to repay you for him, and for the care you have given him these three months."

"My tribe never sells children. But perhaps I want to do you a favor." Liguria coughed again. This time a different young woman entered, carrying a long basket heavy with child which she set down in front of Liguria. Liguria gestured and the young woman moved the basket closer to Alarik, then stood back in the shadows against the wall.

Alarik bent over the infant. It was naked except for a fox tooth amulet hung from a sinew around its neck. He felt vague about how big a three-month-old child should be, and the light was execrable. Certainly he couldn't judge the baby's skin, and Antonia had said nothing about its eyes, but one thing he could see—this infant's head was thatched with as black and shaggy a growth as Lahm's. He looked at Liguria. She watched him impassively. He roughed the child's hair; the child screwed up its face, then laughed. When he withdrew his hand he laid it palm up in his lap; it was clean. Liguria was watching him. Passing his hand reflectively over his mouth he gave it a quick, wet lick and tried again, rubbing the baby's hair hard between thumb and fingers. Again they came away unblackened.

He took out of his pack a package of salt the size of his

two fists and laid it between his feet. "This is payment for the boy I seek," he said.

Even in the bad light he could see her teeth gleam in a brief grin. She said nothing to him but spoke in her own tongue to the young woman standing in the shadows. The young woman took the infant away. Shortly she returned, carrying another, but she hesitated. Alarik saw Liguria's chin lift and the young woman quickly laid the second baby in the basket in front of him. He bent over it. Liguria said something more and the young woman began to light more lamps he hadn't noticed before.

The baby's head was covered with a shine of fine red hair. He was awake; when Alarik moved a finger in front of his face he followed it with eyes as green as Valrada's, as Berto's, as Lord Eurik's. Alarik stroked the fair cheek and the boy smiled. He was less pleased when the finger prodded his stomach. Batting at it, he sucked in his breath to howl; his forehead gathered itself in the middle like Lord Eurik's when he was crossed. Alarik looked up at Liguria and his heart turned over.

She was watching him through narrow eyes; from just below the left one to the corner of her mouth she had a thin white scar.

Seeing him stare, her lips drew back, but only her mouth smiled; her eyes were unreadable. Her face was as wrinkled as a drought-stricken riverbed; she had to be ancient, yet not a tooth was missing from her gums. All were flawless white—all filed sharp as needles. The lamplight gleamed dully on her beads, a string of amber the color of fox eyes.

The perfume from the lamp oil was thickening in the air; he felt that he was being slowly drugged—he had an insane impulse to grab the boy and run.

"I have said that perhaps I wanted to do you a favor," the old woman said softly. "Why not leave your boy with us? Every boy of my tribe learns more of the woods before he is twelve than your king's chief huntsman will ever know. I would teach him things your priests cannot imagine. You would always have us for friends. If you take him, my debt to you is discharged."

She had dropped her voice, but there was nothing sinister in it. Her offer might not be entirely disingenuous, but he knew that to her, the finest soldier in Gaul was a saddle-bumpkin. He chose his grounds for refusal carefully. "The child's father was a Christian—"

She looked at him wisely; he saw she was convinced the baby was his.

"...his mother is a Christian——"

She sat back impatiently. "Christian! Anyone can see the child is a Frank. You can paint a cross on his forehead, and you can pour new wine into old skins, but the same curse is on both. You will never drink such wine, and no one can make Christians out of Franks. For that you need a new people with no gods of their own, and where are they?"

Behind her the family of jars—the extra lamplight showed the human face painted on each lid—stared through him, sightless as the embalmed objects Alarik suddenly realized they contained. He kept his voice level. "I have given his mother my word." He took one last thing, Brunehaut's small bag, out of his open pack, and from it he extracted one gold coin bearing the face of the second Theodosius. He stood up as well as he could and offered Liguria the coin and the salt.

She accepted the salt. "I take this for his food and shelter." He nodded gravely, knowing as well as she how desperately precious salt was to her. "But the child himself is yours; there is no need to buy him."

"It is the law."

"Whose law?"

He had blundered, mentioning usurpers' law to a queen. "I must give it to you or he will have bad luck."

Liguria took the coin and looked at both sides, then dropped it in the hanging pocket where the bracelet had gone. Alarik took the silver chain with its tiny olive-wood crucifix out of Brunehaut's bag and fastened it around her son's neck. He would have preferred to do this after he had parted from Liguria, but Brunehaut had his oath that he would do it the instant her son was in his grasp. Liguria watched ironically. Like the black-haired infant, Brunehaut's also wore a fox's tooth; this Alarik took care not to disturb.

"You could have waited to let the monks put their charm on him," Liguria said. "It will do him no good in the forest."

"If you would wear one of these charms, the monks would give you all the salt you need. Let me carve you one."

"Your kind monks are bears: They want to embrace my race to extinction." She spoke rapidly to the young woman who still stood with her back against the wall, and the young woman hurried behind the curtain. In a moment there was light behind it, and Alarik could hear whispers. The woman came back carrying a rabbit-skin pouch which she gave to him. From its feel the pouch seemed to be full of grist. "Mix a little with water and feed it to him when he cries," Liguria told him.

"Thank you." He nudged Storm's saddle with his foot. "Shall I give you this in return?"

For less than a second she looked good-humored. "Don't throw the rope after the bucket." Her expression was inscrutable again, but he trusted her, laid the baby on the saddle, and picked up both.

When he came out of the earth, he found Storm tethered to the branch the heron had lit on.

XXXVIII

October 16, 585

THE SUN HAD THE SKY ALL TO ITSELF. JUST ONCE, DAG THOUGHT, he would like to say that of himself about something. He let the roan trot along without urging. The priest's reasons for this meeting had seemed to him less than compelling. In a normal October he wouldn't have promised to come at all, he would have been too busy with the grapes. The drought, however, having spared him no grapes to harvest, he did have time on his hands. His late brother's priest ranked a very poor second to Plectrudis of Convenae when it came to filling that time, but there being no way Dag could spend a daylight hour with Plectrudis without scandal, he was on his way to the church. He would be glad when his niece married and Alarik could attend to this priest and his roof and his straw and his oil.

Dag knew the priest was worried that Valrada's

betrothal hadn't been settled. Probably this morning's business was a cover for trying to find out when it would be. Dag planned to substitute hauteur for information, which he lacked. No one had seen Alarik since September, when his brother had come to Dag with some story, as if Dag cared. Dag liked Alarik, but if Dag's niece married a landless man, no one would have to be told she wasn't doing it to please Dag.

No doubt his niece shared the priest's impatience. Imagining the scene at Ste. Croix if she had to be told that Alarik had disappeared, Dag really hoped Alarik's brother's story had been the truth. Meanwhile, until Valrada married *some*body, every time the priest got rheumatism he was going to come to Dag about it.

Riding to what had been his father's church always made Dag melancholy. All but one of his children were buried there, and he missed them, especially when he thought about the one who was left. He really was the unluckiest man ever born. All but one of his sons were dead (and that one not fit to enter his mind this close to a church), while all but one of his wife's brothers lived.

Things were always a little too late for Dag, from the day his mother had born him second. Now Gontram of Burgundy was raising an army from all Gaul to march on Spain. Could anyone doubt that seven months ago Rikimer would have been first to volunteer? Had anyone been hotter for the war in Brittany? Had Dag and his wife combined been able to keep him home when Childebert marched on Paris? Had anyone failed to see Rikimer's expectant, avaricious joy when Tours revolted, when Poitiers rebelled, when the old king's bastard holed himself up in Convenae? Rikimer would have ridden against God's own angels if there'd been a prayer of getting a pasture out of it. Now that Poijou was his in all but law, his interest in fighting ended at Poijou's four corners.

If Eurik could have lived even another seven months, Rikimer right now would be riding for Spain, and Dag wouldn't be constantly sniffing his food, looking over his shoulder. Dag could have remerged Poijou with Antier, instead of having to let Rikimer ensconce himself. (God help him if he hadn't let Rikimer ensconce himself now; Dag glanced over his shoulder.)

Dag didn't have to reproach himself with ever having wished Eurik's death, and certainly not Lady Chrona's. If *Eurik* had lived and *Dag's* wife had died, Rikimer would be on his way to seek his fortune across the blue mountains, and Dag would marry Lehun of Claigne's daughter Theomaka himself. Antier was what Lehun found attractive, not Rikimer. No doubt, Dag began to grin as he jogged along, Lehun would prefer him. He was young enough to beget sons and old enough to die out of their way before they soured in their bottles for being corked too long, as Rikimer had done. He could marry Theomaka, and Plectrudis could be moved out of the weaving women's quarters into a cottage of her own. Lehun's cubs were choirboys compared to Dag's present six brothers-in-law.

Dag trotted south, grinning and grimacing as the possibilities and the facts of his life alternated in his mind. The priest's mongrel heralded Dag's approach from behind the graveyard gate; its yaps rose two pitches as Dag dismounted.

There was another horse tethered in front of the church; a dreadfully scarred black gelding.

One worry less.

The dog's barking brought the priest out; Dag tethered the roan and let the even more than usually nervous holy father usher him through the dark church into a brightly sunshiny side room, where Alarik stood waiting.

Alarik's greeting was so formal and tense that Dag realized at once he had relaxed too soon. He made a show of interest in the room, looking around, not anxious to hear whatever it was these two had got him here for.

The room contained several large chests against the walls; apparently it was the priest's vesting chamber. On top of one of the chests a baby lay sleeping in a basket.

In a drought year like this, foundlings were the biggest crop. The priest knew the routine and needed no more from Dag than his seal on a paper or two. Therefore....

"This child concerns you closely," Alarik said, and uncovered its head. Dag's heart took a queer turn. He shot a look at Alarik's grim face and understood the priest's trepidation.

Valrada, while all of them had been off at war, had had a bastard. Alarik, on learning of it, had disappeared rather than be dishonored by marrying her. Now he'd had second thoughts. Someone had persuaded him that Dag would raise his niece's dowry rather than see her exposed.

Rikimer would never consent to such a concession out of Poijou; it would have to come out of Antier. Dag was sweating furious. Eurik would have killed this insolent landless nobody on the spot, the child next. Dag's head remained bent over the child. If he drew on this younger, bigger man, he was the one who would feed worms. He closed his eyes.

"Your brother's son," Alarik said.

Dag's eyes flew open. He almost laughed his relief. One last bastard whose mother expected something!

Smiling, Dag rubbed the baby's forehead with his thumb. The baby frowned in its sleep, the red star on its forehead puckering as Eurik's scar had used to do. Dag's thumb came away clean. He had known it would, unless the mother was a simpleton. He spit on one corner of the child's cover and rubbed the mark again, harder, but nothing was changed except that the child woke up crying. Dag glanced at Alarik. Alarik, he noted, was watching every move Dag made around the child, as if he half expected Dag to throttle it on the spot. The priest hovered, conciliatory, tense as a cat on a rope bridge. "Who," Dag asked genially, "is the mother?"

"Your brother's wife," said Alarik.

Dag took a step backward.

"He is the son of Lord Eurik and Lady Brunehaut," Alarik repeated.

Dag uncovered the child in two motions. It was male all right. He judged it was some months old; it might have been Eurik's. "Where did you get this child?" he rasped.

"From the midwife your son had bribed to kill it."

Suddenly the priest was at Dag's elbow offering him wine.

Alarik told his story without raising or lowering his voice from beginning to end. The priest had retreated to the furthest corner and sat telling his beads, trying never to let Dag catch him looking up.

"What is the blood price," Alarik asked levelly, "of the man who did this?"

The priest jumped up and left the room.

Dag sat down. The priest must have put the chair behind him at some point; Dag hadn't noticed. "I can't take composition for the killing of my son."

Alarik had not sat down. "You can't refuse justice to the widow of your brother. You're her nearest kin. When the man who kills this murderer in her name is brought to trial, you should be *her* champion, not the murderer's."

"My son has six uncles," Dag said. "Setting composition for his death would not be left all up to me."

"You must tell your son's uncles to set a price Lady Brunehaut's champion can pay or she will petition the king for the justice she cannot get from you."

Dag stood up abruptly and poured himself more wine. He stood looking at it. He drank two swallows and put it down. The child had gone back to sleep. Dag studied its blotched forehead, its red hair, the strangely marked fox's tooth that lay under the crucifix on its chest. The boy might be Valrada's. Alarik might know so, or he might not. Alarik might be its father himself. The boy might be Eurik's. Its mother might be some slave. Dag scowled at the sleeping baby.

"A good bull is half the herd," Eurik had often said, and laughed every time. Dag reached for his wine. Alarik's story might be true. Dag drained his cup. "If Lady Brunehaut petitions the king, who will swear for her?" he asked bluntly. Rikimer, if his kin stood with him, could fill the court with oath-helpers. "Your story must be believed or you, not Rikimer, would be put to the ordeal to test it. I know of no poor man who ever won a trial by ordeal."

"Who that sees its father's face will doubt its father's name?"

Dag looked away. Who but himself realized that his brother had had no birthmark? Who else remembered Eurik before his father had chosen him for Odin and marked him in such deadly secrecy, for fear of the Christian priest, that he had gone to his grave believing Dag himself didn't know what his brother's burn had meant? And if there were a soul on either villa who did remember, would he speak of it, if to do so would deliver both villas into Rikimer's hands? Rikimer, who would tax the dead. Dag looked back at Alarik.

"If you convince Rikimer's uncles of his guilt, I will require that he leave Poijou, that he join the army Gontram is raising against Spain."

Alarik stood frowning and silent.

"All my wife's brothers will be at my hall in two weeks," Dag said, "for the feast of All Saints. Lady Brunehaut and Valrada can be my wife's guests for this feast. The matter of your wedding must wait until this is settled." It made no sense for Valrada to marry a landless man whose neck she and he were hell-bent on risking before her maidenhead, assuming she still had it, stopped bleeding. That was blood Dag could sell to Lehun of Claigne for one of his sons, if Alarik got himself cut down before it flowed. Otherwise, Alarik could have her.

One way or the other, Dag didn't see how he could lose.

XXXIX

November 1, 585

APPROACHING HER UNCLE'S HALL, VALRADA PASSED THE GROUP OF jugglers who were to entertain his guests for All Saints'. Among them she suddenly saw, and felt her stomach lurch as she saw, the dark minstrel who had foretold Antonia's fire; who had sung of the red star shining in the forest—Lord Eurik's infant, but how had he known?

What else did he know?

Could he sing, for instance, about a spear that had broken, and a youth who had died before the quarry the spear had been meant to kill?

It was enough, she had been trying to make herself accept, that they were sure of Rikimer's villainy toward Brunehaut, Brunehaut's son; she should not need to know one way or the other about Berto now.

But she did.

She had no reason, she told herself severely, no reason to believe that the strange minstrel even knew she had ever had more than one brother. She could not, she did not need to tell herself, question him intelligibly in the midst of all those busy-mouthed jugglers.

She took another step toward him and paused, her heart pounding. "Minstrel, how many of my brothers are to be avenged today?"

"Lady—both, or neither."

Valrada turned from him and entered the hall. The first face she saw was the skull Rikimer had worn in his hair as he leaned over the dying Berto. She took her place quickly, to hide her trembling.

Trestles had been dragged into Antier's hall and boards laid on them to make extra tables. The hall was so stuffed with men, women and children, Rikimer was getting warm already and the drinking had barely begun.

Year before last, Rikimer's Uncle Erman had hosted the feast of All Saints at Niort; last November should have been Dag's turn, but they had all been mired down in Paris, so now, in the Year of the Drought, providing the feast fell to Dag, a piece of bad luck over which Rikimer had listened to Dag whine for the last two months. With all the mead, meat, and meal Poijou had contributed to saving Dag from shame, Rikimer might well have been considered the feast's cohost. Aside from that, Rikimer couldn't quarrel with his place, the last at the head table. No man had been seated ahead of him who didn't have documents to more than Rikimer, for the present, could claim in court. Higher were only his father, his six uncles and their wives, Lehun of Claigne, and, seated beside Rikimer, Lehun's stolid lady. (To think that he was angling to hook her as a mother-in-law.) Rikimer's mother, as usual, was denying herself the banquet.

Had she not been at this instant on her knees before Antier's altar, Rikimer would have found himself at the second table—with his friend Wulf, it was true, but also with his "aunt" Brunehaut and several other people whose company he coveted as little, such as Wulf's younger brothers and his own dear cousin Valrada.

Brunehaut was inflicting her lump of a baby on her dinner companions. Rikimer hoped her incredible satisfaction in this daughter consoled her when she remembered, as often she must, how she had brushed him off like mold.

She had cocooned the baby like a larva and sat

clutching it to her more than ample bosom as if just one glance at its face would cause the ravished beholder to snatch the child and run.

There was a pennant hanging point down like a sword directly over Rikimer's head; Dag had all Antier's pennants and flags on display, more than he'd carried against the Pretender. Rikimer's mother had looked at them as if they were nooses and taken to the chapel the way some women take to their beds.

Rikimer's eyes estimated the crowd he was helping, unthanked, to feed. In addition to the head table, which had been pulled parallel to the hearth, improvised trestle tables lined both sides of the far end of the hall. The hall's center was left clear for the tumblers Dag had hired to entertain his guests between courses. Tumblers bored Rikimer and he regretted that he would have no one to talk to when they appeared. Even his priest would have been better than the Lady of Claigne. He was sorry for the priest, jammed in with a lot of Rikimer's youngest cousins halfway down the hall. This was his first feast day since his promotion from deacon, and no doubt he had not forseen that fate.

Rikimer was less sorry for Mark of Vien, who ranked higher, though he had arrived on a gaunt old mule with a face like a Roman abbess. Mark had lost his horses but had paid his debt, to Rikimer, anyway, Rikimer could not imagine how.

Luther of the Bourre had not been so fortunate. Rikimer was surprised he had the stomach to come, in his new circumstances. Rikimer and his newly vested priest had cantered past him trudging north, and there he was, seated lower than the priest, now. He looked like death.

At the head of the table, Dag was on his feet for the

first toast: They would all have to stand. Rikimer sighed; his father's toasts were always humilitatingly labored.

"His Radiant Majesty, Clotar II!"

That was Dag's toast *in toto;* Rikimer's eyebrows went up in spite of himself. Beside him the Lady of Claigne lifted their mutual wine to her fat-smeared lips, took a manly swallow, and handed the goblet to Rikimer. As Rikimer raised it he saw his father frowning toward him, or rather, he quickly corrected that impression, across him. Rikimer swiveled before drinking. At the foot of the next table, Alarik Alansson stood empty-handed and scowling. For a second, Rikimer forgot to drink.

Dag's arm leveled at Alarik. "Why," he did a fair job of thundering, "do you not toast our king?"

The room fell deathly still. Rikimer felt his scalp prickle and he waited for Alarik's answer as he would have waited for a juggler to get himself down from a tightrope. "Because," the answer came, "I cannot drink a usurper's wine!"

Rikimer's head jerked back toward his father. Dag was staring over Rikimer's shoulder at Alarik and Alarik alone as if to look at anyone else would blind him. No one had reseated himself after drinking the king's health. Now there was a scraping of chairs and a quick hubbub, quickly hushed. Rikimer also sat down, reluctantly. He was fascinated, almost more than astounded. What could have moved this slow and close-mouthed follower to march naked alone into a she-bear's cave and commence yelling insults at the bear? He did not look drunk.

"I accuse you," Alarik's words were loud enough to be heard at the far end of the hall, "of taking my oath falsely. Not you but your nephew should be my lord."

For the voice of a raving man, Alarik's was fantastically controlled.

Dag's reply came faster than Rikimer could get his breath. "Produce any nephew. Everyone knows my brother had only one child to survive by each wife, and both were daughters: my niece Valrada——"

Halfway up the table from Alarik, Valrada sprang to her feet. "I am here, and so—" she stretched both arms toward Brunehaut— "is my brother!" Brunehaut had the child unwrapped in readiness; *these three together were staging this.* Rikimer felt the hop in his left cheek awaken as Valrada took the naked child and held—*him*—high for everyone to see. She gave Rikimer one venomous stare he was too stunned to return and then walked around her table out into the hall's empty rectangle and turned slowly with the baby held as high as she could lift it for all in the hall to see.

Dag's guests strained to look. Valrada was barely a spear's length from Rikimer, and the child's red hair and starred forehead were as plain to him as its penis.

"This is Lord Eurik's son," Alarik announced, following Valrada into the open space, "who was drugged and hidden and a servant's daughter put in his place so that even his mother did not know of it."

Rikimer's cheek was leaping wildly. He held his hand to it and looked at his father.

"I am innocent of all this," was his father's answer. Good God, no denial, no questions, no *challenge?* "I was in Paris when Lady Brunehaut gave birth," Dag went on cravenly, *apologetically,* "and I really thought my brother had left a daughter."

Rikimer's cheek threatened to leap out from under his

hand; he lowered his elbow to the table so that he could appear to be leaning negligently on it and pressed harder still.

"But your son was not innocent of it," said Alarik. "He planned and paid: I accuse him."

Rikimer shot to his feet. Halfway down the room, his priest was faster. "*I* accuse him," the priest screamed. "He did all that, and then murdered the doctor he'd paid to do it!" The priest was one scream from hysteria. Jerking off the cross Greek Nicolaus had given him, he brandished it at Rikimer. "You killed him, devil from hell, you poisoned him! Murderer!" he sobbed. *"Usurer!"*

Rikimer's gut attacked him with a burning spasm; he gripped the table edge till he could speak. "I deny it. By the rim of the shield, I did not. By the withers of the horse, by the point of the sword, I did none of these things." He tried to conceal his gasping need for more air. "This child may be my uncle's; I know nothing of it. Ask the man who told the first lie, and ask my cousin there beside him, if the child is their own?"

"I anticipated this slander," Valrada answered. "Last night I went to my aunt—*your mother*," she faced Rikimer triumphantly, and Rikimer saw she was trembling. "I told her some question might arise before my wedding because I have been fatherless so many months." She managed to sound so pathetic Rikimer choked. "I was examined last night by the Lady of Antier herself, and her midwife and her sisters-in-law, Lady Bertrud and Lady Monegunda. I am a virgin, and when the duke comes to try you, I will submit myself to any four married women he may name."

Beside Dag, Rikimer's oldest uncle's wife looked first at

his Aunt Monegunda and then at her husband. None of them looked at Rikimer. Lady Bertrud rose shakily and after one frightened glance in Dag's direction—but none in Rikimer's—faced the hall. "She is a virgin," Lady Bertrud said, and sat down.

Rikimer realized he was freezing.

If his mother were there, she could help him. As always when he needed her, she was elsewhere trying to wash Christ's feet and there was no one to help him. So Valrada had kept herself, and the child was some slave's bastard. Bad luck, but if his mother were here she would lie for him, she could save him. Any normal mother would lie to save her son. Not Bertrud, but his mother, would have answered Valrada, and Bertrud and Monegunda would not have challenged his mother if she had lied. Rikimer's brain kicked at his skull. "This child is not my uncle's wife's," he said. "Now before God I speak and He knows if I lie: I know nothing of the crimes I am charged with. I deny each and all."

"Liar!" shouted Alarik. "How many oath-helpers will support your lie?"

Only the table-length from Rikimer, his father sat as if his arms were bound to his sides. His eyes stared doggedly at his goblet. His wife's six brothers were rigid, watching him. At the next table Wulf stood up, but at some sign from their father, his brothers pulled him back into his seat, and after one glance at his father's face, Wulf didn't rise again. He sat, hunched, head down over his plate. In the crowded Hall, Rikimer saw no man stand for him, though many watched his father, his uncles, and would have stood if they had not abandoned him. His mother, his mother if she were here, her brothers, his father, they could not sit there if she were here, they could never sit there before her eyes. Rikimer's heart pounded in his throat.

Dag's eyes were slowly rising, but to Alarik's. "How many oath-helpers support your charge?"

There was a movement at the lowest table, as if anyone cared whether any of that chaff stood or rolled on the floor. Rigid, Rikimer saw his priest, he had expected that; Alarik's brother, of course; Mark of Vien; Odo Lehunsson—for a second Rikimer's sight blurred but it cleared and focused on his father as Dag began to speak again. "Before God I swear I knew nothing of this." Dag turned both hands palm up like a man showing that he holds no weapon. Sweat shone on his forehead. "I knew nothing of Lady Brunehaut's son till now.

"I will restore Poijou to my brother's son, and ask the duke to name his regent. I will commend my son to King Gontram, to serve him against the heretics in Spain."

As Dag's words came so smooth, so ready, Rikimer realized the extent of his betrayal. "Commend your stinking whore," he screamed. "This is a conspiracy!" His fingers fumbled wildly with his scabbard. "I declare my innocence and call God to judge!" With sword drawn, he rushed at Alarik.

The charge was what Alarik had told Brunehaut and Valrada to pray for. He threw Skull-smasher in patent self-defense before all Rikimer's kindred, and God judged Rikimer guilty.